1

"Can you tell me how it happened?"

The question rings in my mind. It is a straightforward question, but one that comes with a lengthy answer. Could I though? Yes. I could tell it all as though it was happening right now, with every detail, every action, every moment just as fresh as they were when I experienced them. Yes. I could tell our story easily.

"It would take me a long time to tell it all." I say with my tired eyes focused on the eager face before me.

"You know I have time."

The words seem to smile, but there is a sense of pain behind them. I take a deep breath, and glance out the window as all of the memories crowd my mind. Despite the way my body has worn, my memories are as vibrant as ever. I settle in for what I expect will be a long night, closing my eyes tight as I begin to speak.

"They called us Zosimos, the survivors. The few, the strong, and the lucky. It's true that they weren't many of us there; it's true that we were strong. We had to be in order to survive. As for lucky, well some thought that we would all have been better off if we had died with the others. The majority of us then were ninth or tenth generation Zosimos, and we, were all that was left.

It had been many years since The Attack, but even then vast areas of the land that remained were still lost to ruin. They told us that there used to be more, much more, but The Attack had swept over land and sea, like a plague, like a swarm of locust. The animals, the people, the trees, were all destroyed. It left behind nothing. Our ancestors were the only ones who lived through it all. They were saved by a man who gave them refuge deep within caves in the side of a cliff. This man called his underground haven The Durga. When they emerged, the people found the landscape to be desolate and stripped of everything they had ever known. All that was left of the world was a small island off the coast of a land called "Europe" by the people of old. That other land vanished along with the rest of the world. The small island was then surrounded by nothing but water as far as the eye could see.

The man that had saved the people used what he called thaumaturgy, a strong force that he possessed, to help them start a new life. It took almost all of his power to make the land able to sustain them once again, but although the people now had sources of food and fresh water, conditions were still not as they had been. There were still ruins of the civilization that preceded the Zosimos covering most of the landscape, making spreading out difficult. Though he tried to rid the land of this debris, before the man was able to finish his work, he became ill. As powerful as he was, he couldn't revive himself. He had used too great an amount of his magic making the island livable again. He soon died, and with him died his power. Despite the great loss of their leader, the Zosimos were able to carry on and continued to build up the nation that they called, Nirvana.

Nirvana was divided into two regions. Aject was in the north, and there was Woden in the south. The capital of Scheol, consisted of a grand palace, that sat in Northern Aject. A small portion of Aject stretched down Woden's eastern side along the coast. Being close to Scheol gave those in Aject an advantage of wealth. Though their accommodations were finer than those of Woden, Scheol was the only truly wealthy place in Nirvana. Only those that made up the government resided there. King Fino sat in the protection of his palace and ruled the nation. He sent his men, consisting of the Allure and the Enlighteners out to work for him amongst the people. Some spoke of a time when he used to travel around and visit Aject and Woden, but illness left him incapable of such excursions after a while. There were other rumors too though, rumors that the once beloved ruler of Nirvana had long since passed. To some, this meant we should no longer have to abide by the rules that were put in place during his reign. Such talk generally came from those with nothing better to do than to gossip.

My family and I lived in the middle of the Woden region. Back then it would have taken us at least ten days to reach the border of Aject from where we lived, and even longer to reach any people. For miles between the regions, there was nothing but densely treed forests. A large portion of that forested area became known as the Melaine Forest. Within those trees were various ruins that had long since been overcome by their surroundings. There were tales of more that just ruins lurking in the shadows though. Horrible creatures, all with a thirst for blood, trees that would come alive, ground that would swallow a man whole, and plants that had the power to kill with a single touch. Beyond there were more forests, nothing like Melaine, but still dangerous in their own ways. A single road ran from the far south through the forests up to the place where Aject met Scheol. The few that dared travel the road were the ones who relayed the stories of the horrors of Melaine to the rest of us. Those stories did a fair job of keeping others out.

Woden City was the main area of the Woden region and its sister city was that of the grand city of Aject. Most of the population of Woden resided in the city or just around it. The smaller shops and businesses were scattered around among the large city buildings, but the factories and mills were more spread out with houses surrounding them. The government provided almost everything that we had, clothes, running water, and they kept our stores full of food.

"Working together for the betterment of Nirvana." was our national motto, and we worked all right. Nine to ten hours a day for most. We started working at the age of seven. Children spent six hours a day in school learning about our nations history, and some simplified work skills. Seven was no age for a child to start work, but those were different times.

The work we did varied from factory work, from work in the forest hunting and gathering to work for those few who owned their own small shops. Well, "owned", being a relative term. Half of whatever that shop owner made would be collected in the weekly Sweep, and that money went to "the betterment of Nirvana". Those who owned shops often joked about the amount of money that the government took from them. The reality was that they got that money back through other things that were provided by our rulers, but there was no convincing them of that at the time.

My father was one such shop owner. He and I ran his blacksmith shop, and growing up wielding the tools, such an occupation required, made me strong. I was one of the lucky ones, never having been forced to work in one of the many different factories or mills. I also never had to work in the forest, hunting and gathering, although I wouldn't have minded learning to hunt. My father made sure that on my seventh birthday when the officials came around to assign me a job that I was assigned to his shop. My two older brothers were not as lucky. The law used to be that families could not have their own children working for them. I suppose that was because the government wanted to make sure that no one was receiving special treatment. It wasn't until the year before I turned seven that the law was changed.

Working in the shop was hard work, and my father put a large amount of responsibility on me. I became skilled at making many different kinds of weapons. I could start a fire with considerable ease, having done it hundreds of times in the mornings before we began working. I did it far more in the winter when we had to have more than one source of heat in order to last until the seasons changed. The downside to working in the shop was that I didn't get to see too many people. There were the occasional moments when my father was in the middle of working with a piece that was fresh out of the fire, and he sent me to help a customer. Even then, most of those customers were officials coming for weapons. As for anyone close to my age, well, most days I was lucky to see anyone under the age of thirty.

Still, I took pride in the fact that I could make just about anything. My father taught me well in the ten years I spent there.

During that time, I rarely was clear of dirt and soot. After a day of work, my blonde hair would look almost black from my constant attempts to brush it from my face as I worked. I hardly looked like myself at times. Black marks accumulated on my face and neck from trying to wipe off the sweat that was caused by the intense heat of the fire in the small shop. I could spend an hour scrubbing my body with a wet cloth every night, but it was useless. The black lines under my fingernails seemed as though they would never fully vanish.

My mother tried her best to help make things easier on us whenever she was able. She was able to get a job cleaning the homes of the many officers that lived in Woden and she was adept. She was fortunate enough to work only about six hours a day, and when she came home she catered to the needs of the rest of us. She always wanted us to look presentable wherever we went. She did not care that others would think nothing of our family showing up dirty, clothes. Still, we all did our best to comply with her wishes. My mother was the most beautiful woman I had ever seen. She had beautiful dark hair that went all the way down to the small of her back, but her outward beauty was only half of it. Her constantly positive and sweet spirit made up the other half.

Reg, my eldest brother, was twenty-nine at the time. He was blessed with fine looks like my mother, but he was also blessed with height and strength. His dark hair and brown skin along with his smooth personality had girls all over Woden swooning for years, but only Phoibe was able to steal his heart. When they got married my mother was able to get Phoibe a job change to work alongside her, cleaning houses.

Reg worked in the forest, and although hunting was a useful skill, it could be incredibly dangerous. Hunting takes precision and skill, and Reg was once one of the most skilled hunters in Woden. He was incredible with a bow. He could take down a deer with an arrow to the head from distances that to all others would have been impossible, but he lost his right hand in a knife incident. When it happened we were all scared he would never work again. Reg wasn't one to let anything get him down though, not for long anyway. For three months after the incident Reg trained with a sword, he was determined to work again whatever it took. It did take him a while to get the hang of things, but eventually he was just as capable as anyone with both their hands. He didn't stop at that though. He taught himself to throw knives with incredible accuracy as well, and he also learned how to set a variety of deadly traps. Only five months had gone by before Reg was back at work and better than ever.

Reg was one of the most resolved people I'd ever known. He had the strength to overcome even what seemed to be the greatest of obstacles but being strong all the time wore on him. He could be so thoughtful, and he was an extraordinarily influential speaker, but he had a problem with drinking his. He often would drink his pain away, and that created division between him and the rest of our family.

One night not long after he lost his hand I was up late to watch an eclipse that the whole city had been going on about, Clem had fallen asleep, and as I turned to wake him up I noticed Reg stumbling down the street. I watched as he lost his balance and fell in a heap on the ground.

"Reg!" I said rushing to his side, "Reg what's wrong?" Instantly I could smell the alcohol on his breath. As drunk as he had gotten in the past, I'd never seen him allow himself to get that. "Reg?"

My voice was trembling, and I rose to go wake Clem for help, Reg grabbed my arm.

"Ell…I can't, I can't…" He stuttered in a hushed voice, "She's going to leave Ell. Phoibe…She won't stay. Not when she can have him. Orfeo, he did this to me." He said as he held up his right arm. "I can't take care of her now, I'm nothing. Look at me. I can't even take care of myself, much less anyone else." Tears were streaming down his face as he whispered, "Rona…I'm sorry Rona."

I was so shocked to see him like that I couldn't even speak. Of course he could take care of Phoibe. She wouldn't leave him for the world. As for Rona, I know he loved her with all his heart, we all did, and he had no reason to be sorry. "What happened to Rona wasn't your fault Reg. Do you hear me Reg? There is nothing you could have done to help her."

"Nothing I could have done!?!" Reg said in a serious voice as he looked at me with sorrowful eyes, tainted with anger. "Aella. That day, I promised her that I'd be there. I promised that I'd walk them home. I forgot. I fell asleep and didn't show up." He could hardly speak between the tears and he was slurring his words.

I couldn't find the right words to say in order to console him. So instead I helped him to his feet and around the house to get him some water. I attempted to wash his face as he continued to sob. After a few minutes, Clem approached, his face asked all of his questions instantly. My answer to was a nod of the head and he joined me at Reg's side. As he sat there he allowed the alcohol to take over and refused to get up and go into the house. It took all of the strength Clem and I had to lift and carry him into the house. We placed him gently on his cot next to Phoibe's. He had stopped crying by that point thankfully so we were able to do all of this without making too much noise.

I made a promise to myself that night that I would never tell anyone of what had happened. Clem knew that Reg was drunk, and I decided to let that be all he would ever know. I made him swear he would never ask Reg about it, though I imagined Reg would have no recollection of the night's events. I never was able to see Reg the same after that. I still was strength, but I also saw weakness that made me worry about him.

Clem was twenty-one then, and he worked at the lumber mill. He came home most days with bad back pain from all the lifting and cutting that his job required. Unlike most of the workers at the mill, he came home to a mother like ours. She massaged his back every night until his stiff muscles released their tension. I worried about him still. He was small for his age and wasn't necessarily attractive. He was the only member of our family with red hair, and he stood out a great deal. He had no shortage of muscle and what he lacked in height and looks he sure made up for with his personality. His sense of humor was unmatched. He took after my father with his kind and understanding nature.

Clem and I were close, a great deal more so than Reg and I. When we were kids we did everything together. We had an unspoken understanding of one another that neither of us could explain. He always called me Ell. Since he was only four when I was born, he had a hard time with my name. He only really called me Aella when something was wrong, or when he was angry with me.

I was scared for a time that Reg and Clem would resent me somewhat for my job, but as I got older I was able to see how understanding they were. They were always looking out for me as I was for them. We had to be close in order to make it through. We all did."

I stop as the memory of my home in Woden flashes before my eyes, and I let out a sigh as I gaze through the window until the sound of a soft voice brings me back to the present.

"You don't have to go on if you wish not to. If it makes you sad, then I don't want…"

"I'm not sad. It's just that I haven't really thought it about it all in a long, long time." I respond with an even tone. "It's a strange feeling."

"It's all very important to you, isn't it? Every detail means something?"

"Yes. A story isn't a story without details. Details allow a story to be real and tangible." I answer plainly.

"Well, I want to hear every single one."

"Very well." I say kindly. I open my mouth again, and the words pour from my mouth with such ease I start to forget that I am even telling a story.

2

I awake with a start, my breathing heavy. I have been sweating, so I kick off my blanket, thin as it is. It appears to be just before dawn, as the sky outside the window has a slight pink haze that says the sun will be rising soon. Muggy summer air hangs in the room. Sitting up I look around. Reg and Phoibe are still asleep on their cots that sit about ten feet away from me against the opposite wall of the room we share. I jump a little when I turn to find Clem sitting up on his cot that lies parallel to mine.

"Bad dream?" He asks in a concerned voice, but he doesn't even need to ask because he already knows.

"Same as always." I answer with a slight shrug.

"How can you have the same exact dream every single night of your life? Hell, how do you even remember your dreams? I have dreams, but I always forget what they were about as soon as I wake up."

"I don't know, but it's never even the slightest bit different, and it's all so real. I'm running, and something is chasing me, all the way to the coast. I can't swim to get away because all there is out there is miles and miles of water. I'd drown if I tried it, so I stop and I'm consumed by it. The dream gets more vivid every time I have it." I say, then I look up to see that Clem has an almost amused expression in his eyes.

"What part of that is amusing to you Clem?" I demand a little too loudly apparently because Reg stirs a bit on his cot. "I'm serious." I say, quieter now.

"I'm sorry Ell but really every time you tell me about that dream it seems even more ridiculous, besides you've never even been to the coast."

"I've heard about it, and why is that the only thing you can focus on? As if the rest of the dream is based on reality."

"Sorry…Why don't you try to dream up a way to escape, or something to fight or kill whatever it is. I mean if it's so real and you have it every single night you'd think after a while…" Clem whispers back to me.

"You can't just kill darkness with a sword or gun, Clem…"

"Darkness, Ell?"

"Darkness, that's what it is, at least that's all I see before it swallows me. And it's not like I haven't tried to think of some way to defeat it. I have. As I run I look for someone or something that could help me, but there are only trees that seem to go on endlessly in every direction. The only break from them comes when I reach the shoreline, and there is nothing but miles of sand there, then the water."

As I recall the dream, I twist the ring on my right index finger. The ring was a gift from my father on my twelfth birthday, he fashioned it out of an old key. When he gave it to me, he had said; "Aella, you hold the key to choices in your life, big or small, the power to change your future lies in you." I used to believe it too. I always twist my ring when I am anxious or scared, and Clem knows that full well.

"Ell, I wasn't trying to make light of it, I swear I didn't mean anything by what I said." He puts his hand on my shoulder to comfort me but removes it almost instantly because of how bad I'd been sweating. "It's nothing I should joke about. Sorry." He tries to smile and begins to settle down to go back to sleep.

"It's cold." I say after a moment of looking around the room.

"What in here? Are you kidding, the bloody place is hotter than ever." Clem responds sleepily.

"No not here, the darkness." I whisper, then almost to myself add, "It's cold, freezing cold."

"Try and get back to sleep Aella." Clem says as he drifts off.

I sigh, but although I lie back down and try, I do not go back to sleep. I close my eyes and try to force myself to rest, but my mind keeps racing. Instead, I lie there staring up at the ceiling thinking of ways to evade the darkness the next time I am forced to encounter it. Being so lost in thought, I don't even notice when Reg, Clem, and Phoibe get up and leave the room when morning comes. I am finally roused from my dazed state by my fathers voice calling to me from the kitchen. Only then do I look to the window and realize how late I am. Throwing on my clothes I race out of my room, through our small house and across the lawn and the street into my father's workshop.

"Father I am so sorry!" I call out as I stumble through the open door. Then I quickly begin to pull on my apron and gloves.

"Reg said he spoke to you when he got up this morning." My father replies, calm as ever. "Why didn't you get up the way you normally do? Being late is so unlike you Aella. Is everything okay?" He glances at me, and my expression answers for me. Thankfully he decides to pretend he didn't notice and changes the subject. "Well, you missed breakfast you know. Good stuff too, your mother worked hard." He continues as he looks over the list of orders for the day.

My father is an even-tempered and good-humored man, similar to Clem. He is strong as an ox and his skills as a blacksmith are unmatched as he learned from his own father, who was the best of his time. The officials around Woden look upon him with respect, as they make up the vast majority of his customers.

I know teaching his only daughter the tricks of his trade probably wouldn't have been his first choice. I'm sure he'd rather have Reg or Clem for the job, but he doesn't show it. I decided a long time back that if he was going to make things work despite what he would have wanted, I was going to work extra hard to prove myself. Sure, I'm not big like Reg or as strong as Clem, but I am a fast learner.

It certainly isn't like me to be late considering how badly I wish to impress my father. So in order to make up for lost time I resolve to stay focused and work extra hard today.

"Sorry Father. It won't happen again, I promise."

"It's alright, but we have our work cut out for us today. Everything has to be done by midhour, there is a meeting in town tonight, and I know that your mother will want us to wash up before we go anywhere."

"We'll never be able to finish all of this by then." I say as I look over the long list in my hand.

"Lucky for us someone was up early working to put us ahead." My father replies as he takes the list and begins to cross items off.

"Father, if I'd known that…Well, that's no excuse, but…"

"Just get to work so we aren't late tonight." He smiles once more and gives me a light pat on the back.

I wonder a moment though about the meeting that he mentioned. Such a thing is uncommon in Woden, almost nonexistent to my knowledge. From what I'd heard, when there was a meeting called in the past most chose not to attend, and children never did.

"Well I suppose you don't have to go if you don't want to." My father says, noticing the look on my face.

"I thought children didn't have to go." I respond.

"I didn't know you were a child." My father raises an eyebrow.

"Well, it could be interesting I suppose." I shrug, tinkering with an old hammer.

"I just thought it might be time for you to start doing more adult things." He gives a light laugh. "But Aella, I don't know how you define interesting, but a meeting is going to be more of a serious thing. You really do need to get out more."

"I might if my boss didn't have me working from sun up to sun down." I give him a sarcastic glance.

"Oh if only I really was the one who made the rules, but if you wish to have it, the night is yours. Your mother and I will be fine to go to the meeting ourselves."

"You don't suppose Reg and Phoibe will join? Or Clem?" I say. "I mean if all of them are going then I might as well."

"Well fine, but you realize that Koen is going to have to come along if you do."

"I'll look after him." I say quickly. "I promise."

"Wonderful. Now, if you don't mind getting your lazy self to work, we might actually make it to town before the meeting it over." My father laughs, and I can't help but smile to myself.

The day is long, but the work is relatively easy. As soon as we finish, we head back to the house to clean up. When we round the corner of the house we find my mother standing against the wall, washrag in hand.

"Don't either of you even dare think about setting foot in this house before you get that dirt off of you." She says, folding her arms over her chest. My father and I can't help but laugh as we both make a joking dash towards the door.

"Elias!" My mother calls as she the washrag at his back.

"Fine." He responds, picking up the rag from the ground, and rubbing it quickly over his face. "Now I'm clean." He smiles as he proceeds to march through the door followed by my mother who is doing her best not to seem amused.

* * * * *

As my family and I walk into the town square together, we notice several dozen Allure officers spread throughout the square. It isn't as if the citizens of Woden are not accustomed to Allure officers, but these are different. The unusual amount of armor that they wear seems to be catching the attention of everyone in the square. They are armed to the teeth, and virtually the only things visible are their mouths, each of which is pulled into a tight expressionless line. Not only that, but these officials also appear to be a great deal bigger than the ones we are used to. Each of them has a gun that, like the officers, look larger and more powerful than any I have ever seen. The dark outfits, expressionless faces and large guns give them an eerie look that makes me a little uneasy, and I'm not the only one who seems concerned.

Some of the officers are standing in front of the makeshift stage that workers have fashioned in the center of the square. It's a small stage with only just enough room for the eight chairs that line the back of it and a small wooden podium with the Nirvana national emblem carved carefully in the front.

Several city officials sit in the chairs on the stage. Among them is the governor, a stout man of fifty-three. He has kind eyes, and on his round chin he wears a thick brown beard with small tinges of gray spread throughout it. Behind the governor stand two of his advisors, both tall, worn looking men. Next to the mayor sits the head of the Woden officers. I recognize him from my fathers shop. His name is Ailish. His weary gray eyes look off into the distance, and the corners of his mouth are pulled into a slight frown. For a man of forty, he looks as though he could be in his early sixties. This is a result of the fact that his job is very demanding, and it wears on him physically and emotionally. Often he is required by law to arrest and punish a friend and he loses sleep over it. He tries to keep the citizens of Woden out of trouble, and when we do find our way into it, he does whatever he can to defend us. Before he was made an official his life was much happier, but as time has gone on he has been forced to be virtually emotionless, or at least has learned to mask his emotions. Ailish used to visit out home, as well as the shop since he and my father were extremely close, but he was never the same after he was forced to imprison his own wife, who died there. His twelve years of service have treated him more like thirty.

Four familiar officers stand near Ailish talking quietly amongst themselves. As my eyes make their way across the stage they find several figures that are familiar to them, but they also find some that they do not recognize. One that grabs my attention is an unusually tall and slim man with dark hair dressed in a majestic purple suit that is nothing like anything I've ever seen. It is particularly elaborate. The entire thing is embellished with intricate black stitching, and there are black cuffs at the end of each sleeve that appear to be made of velvet, an expensive fabric I have only encountered a few times before. He stands near the rear of the stage, slightly separated from the others. His youthful, clean-shaven stern face surveying everyone as they come into the square. I walk, but keep my eyes fixed on him, then suddenly he turns and his piercing green eyes become locked on mine. People brush past me as I remain unmoved.

As I look at him a strange feeling washes over me, and time begins to feel as though it is slowing down. I start to think that the feeling is terribly familiar, but before I am able to place it someone hits me from behind, causing me to stumble forward, breaking my gaze with the man on stage. In an attempt to regain my balance, I fall into a couple that quickly looks at me with distain. After apologizing I turn to find a boy about my age, perhaps a little older, looking down at me.

"Watch out." He mumbles as he vanishes into the small crowd of people around us. Before I can really react Clem emerges beside me.

"Aella, here you are! Why'd you stop?"

Seeing the look of confusion on my face he grabs my arm not waiting for my answer and ushers me along to where the rest of our family is waiting. My mother grabs me immediately, and starts off on how worried she's been about me.

My mother hasn't always been such an anxious person, when I was younger she let me go virtually anywhere by myself. Now she won't even let me go to the market alone. I can't imagine I was away for more that a minute or two, but I don't say anything. I accept my mothers embrace as she whispers in my ear.

"I just don't want anything to happen to you, Aella."

It wasn't until Rona and Koen that she got this way. Rona and my younger brother Koen were twins. One day when they were only six they were walking home from school when they were attacked. My mother was worried sick and we were all out looking for them. We had just returned when the officers showed up at our home to tell us the news. One of them explained that he and his partner had found the twins while on their evening rounds. Rona was dead when they found her and Koen was barely hanging on. They took him instantly to the infirmary and Rona to their headquarters where Ailish took over her body. We spent the next few days sitting in the small infirmary room, waiting, wishing and praying that Koen would be okay. The days began to feel like weeks. Then finally Asa and Jalen, the doctors, came out and gave us some real news.

"Although Koen will live, he will never be able to speak again. The damage to his nerves is very severe, he has lost the ability to use a large portion of his brain. It'll be a miracle if he walks again. As for him ever being able to go back to school or work in the future, well, I'm afraid that will be impossible. Too much stress on his brain would be detrimental to his already shaky health. I truly am sorry, but our supplies are limited. It was just too late by the time he was brought to us to do anything substantial to prevent this. It's really very strange though, the damage to his body suggests a very large animal is responsible for the attack, yet I found traces of a strange form of venom in his blood." Jalen told us.

Asa said that the wounds that Koen had suffered were unlike any she had ever seen in her thirty some years of infirmary work. She was sure that some sort of animal caused the attack, but she was unsure of a species with the ability to do the damage that this one did.

"Koen is lucky, incredibly lucky." Asa assured us as she led my family and me back to the room where Koen was.

My parents had been allowed back once before, but, for the rest of us, it was the first time to see him. It was the hardest thing I'd ever done. His face was whiter than the moon, and he sat motionless on a cot in the small white-walled infirmary operation room. Koen's whole body was covered in deep cuts and scratches, the most severe damage being on his right side. The worst cut ran from just underneath his right ear all the way down his neck and on to his chest, and his scar from it is a constant reminder of how fortunate he is to have survived.

His skinny body looked even more hopelessly small now than ever. The only real color on his whole body was the redness caused by inflammation around his many wounds. The worse wounds were wrapped in shreds of cloth acting as bandages, but due to the lack of material available the less cumbersome ones were left bare, and still the less severe ones were serious enough to make me sick.

As hard as it was to see Koen, it did nothing to prepare me to see Rona. The sight that awaited us at the morgue that night was almost too much. Rona, my sweet baby sister hardly resembled herself anymore. Her once beautiful face was contorted, and her gorgeous brown hair was crusted in blood, and I had to turn away. The sight haunted me for months afterwards, and I spent many nights crying. Reg took it the hardest though. I would wake up at least three nights a week to the sound of him screaming her name and crying that he was sorry. I didn't find out until the night of the eclipse why he felt so terribly about the whole thing. He felt like he was responsible for the loss of Rona and the horrific condition the incident had left Koen in. That was when he started drinking.

What exactly happened to them the day of the incident we still don't know for sure. We have tried to get Koen to tell us something, but it is often too painful for him. I can't blame Koen though, he tries so hard to be strong, but I know he struggles every moment of every day. He is surely a miracle though, he can walk again, unsteadily, but he can walk. He is tremendously proud of himself for that as are the rest of us. As a twelve year old, his mind makes it so that he acts like he is closer to seven or eight. When the officials came to assign him to a job they decided he was useless and even the easiest job would be hard for him to do, and someone would have to be watching him at all times. So instead he follows my mother and Phoibe around most of the time, but even when he goes along with them, he ends up spending a vast amount of his time sitting alone.

"Aella, where did you go?" My father asks.

As I begin to answer Koen rushes to me and wraps his arms around my waist. He backs up and smiles at me to let me know he's happy I am okay. He then scowls and shakes his finger at me to let me know I worried him. I ruffle his dark curly hair and pull him close to my side.

Just then a drum sounds and the hum of the crowd grows softer as we all shift our attention to the stage. A dull silence hangs in the air as we wait for the governor to rise and make his way to the podium; instead the thin man in the purple suit begins to move slowly forward. A murmur sweeps through the audience as people turn to each other and begin asking questions. How did they not notice him before I wonder, I sure did. He is at least a full head and shoulders taller that the rest of the people on stage and his suit makes him stick out even more.

"He's back…" I hear a man to my right say a little under his breath.

I turn to my father in search of some sort of answer to who this man is, but his face is filled with an equal amount of confusion.

"Elias." My mother says, her voice trembling slightly as she utters my father's name.

"I know." He responds and returns his worried eyes to the stage. Reg, Phoibe, and Clem are all exchanging glances. Reg sees the look of my face and whispers in my ear.

"He's been here before. Eleven years ago was the last time if I remember correctly. He came to announce a rule change. Father says that is what he always comes for, but normally things get bad after he visits. When he came last, he told us of the work law change where kids were then allowed to work for their parents."

"That doesn't sound like something bad to me."

"Yeah well you probably don't remember but along with that law change came more officers. He hung around town for a few weeks himself, and saw twenty-five families killed for various offenses. He also had Ailish tortured for not prosecuting those families, that's part of the reason he looks so old now, it was rough." Reg finishes his story just as the man makes his finally slow step to the podium. He clears his throat and looks over his small audience with his unblinking snake like eyes.

"Well now" The man begins right as his eyes once again find mine, but he peels them away as he continues, "As I'm sure most of you are aware, my name is Damon." His deep, booming voice fills the air and hangs menacingly there long after he closes his mouth.

He has an accent, and I know he has to be from the far northern region of Nirvana. All those that come from Scheol or the majority of northern Aject all share the same accent. They speak in a mildly harsh sounding manor, putting a stronger emphasis on many of their words and letter. Once the resounding of his voice off the many buildings in the square ceases, he continues.

"It appears to me that some of your neighbors did not get the message about a meeting here today. Would anyone like to explain why people have neglected to show up?" He waits for a moment, but everyone remains silent. "Is it not polite to follow orders in this region? Is it not custom to attend meetings when called?" Another silence follows his words.

"No matter I suppose, we shall just continue without them." He gives a wicked smile. "They'll wish they did not miss this I can guarantee that. But back to business yes? I am an Enlightener. I bring you news from the palace at Scheol. King Fino has sent me to bring you the latest list of laws and regulations for Woden. Cari?"

Damon gestures to the group of the other unfamiliar figures on the stage. When he does this a beautiful, dark skinned, pixie of a girl emerges from behind them carrying a black scroll.

3

Everyone in the audience gasps at the sight of her. I take it that Cari is someone new to everyone. She has confidence that seems to be beyond her years, holding herself in a poised and upright manor. She is thin like Damon, and her features are defined and stunning, she wears a purple gown of silk that hangs off just one of her thin shoulders and flows as she walks. The sunlight reflecting off the fabric makes it appear even more spectacular. Her midnight black hair is done up in an elaborate bun with two small curled strands of it hanging down just in front of her ears. She has purple makeup to match her dress heavily applied to her eyelids. The makeup brings out her eyes, which are the same stunning green as Damon's. A rich, red gloss graces her perfect lips, and they stand out against her dark skin.

Damon turns to acknowledge her as she comes forward, and she does so in the same methodically slow manner in which Damon did. His head turned to the side, I notice a tattoo on the right side of his neck. Just above the collar of the purple shirt he wears under his suit. It is an eye-catching red flame about two inches long, and about an inch wide.

"Thank you Cari." Damon says as the girl reaches him and hands over the scroll. She bows slightly before tuning swiftly to leave, when she does I notice her tattoo, a flame, hers is smaller than his but just as red.

Not a sound fills the square as Damon begins to read off the list of laws, all of which are familiar to me as I've seen them plenty of times in the bulletin we receive every Sun's Day. He gets through them all and from what I can tell there weren't any changes, and I'm not the only one that seems to think this. The murmurs start up again, but Damon ends them by calling into the microphone.

"Citizens! Quiet please." He pauses before continuing, a hush falls over the audience, and it is so quiet you could hear a sewing needle hit the ground. "Better. Now, I will tell you that there have been no changes to the laws, but there simply has been an addition." He stops again, causing us to all lean in a little closer awaiting his words with bated breath.

"Well, now that I have your full, undivided attention the new laws are as follows. Children, no matter what age that currently hold positions working in their families business will now be required to spend every other day alternating between working at a factory or in the forest learning the ways of those professions. Factory, Mill, and Forest workers, you will also rotate jobs. The weekly bulletin will contain the schedule for these rotations." Before we can react he quickly adds, "And," He has us locked on him.

"And, any children under the age of sixteen that cannot do or do not have a job, no matter their circumstances are to be taken to Scheol for a brief time. No need to worry, King Fino simply would like a chance to become acquainted with our new generation. If the families of those children would remain in the square, loading that will take place as soon as the transportation vehicles arrive. I would highly recommend that you don't try to run. We will find you and bring you back. If I have to come find you, I will not take you in a kind manner. I have a tight schedule. As for the rest of you, you are dismissed to your homes. Let your neighbors know that if they wish to live, they should be quick about making an appearance here. Thank you for your time and remember that we are working together for the betterment of Nirvana."

I hardly hear his last few sentences. Koen would be taken to Scheol. The thought of it makes my chest grow tight, I feel as though the wind has been knocked out of me. Questions flood my mind. What will become of him? Will he live? If they don't plan to kill everyone will they kill him anyway due to how extreme his disability is? My family members seem to all have the same questions for when I turn to them their eyes are filled with tears and uncertainty.

My mother lets out a horrified shriek and crumbles to the ground crying. My father rushes to her side as she beats the stones of the street. He tries to tell her that it is going to be all right, but she starts to yell, causing a scene as the families fortunate enough to be leaving intact are headed out too quickly to notice her.

"We already almost lost him once Elias! How can you say it's going to be okay? My baby...not another one of my babies..."

I look to Koen, and although I see the fear in him, he smiles his sweet kindly smile at me and nods his head as if to tell me that he is going to be okay. I rush to him and wrap him tightly in my arms. We both cry and I keep telling him over and over how much I love him and that everything will be alright. My sobs are loud but as Koen cries his tears just fall silently from him eyes. Clem, Reg, and Phoibe all gather around Koen and take turns hugging him, each of their faces stained with tears. When Koen hugs Phoibe he holds on as tight as he possibly can, as the tears begin to fall even harder from his innocent eyes.

Almost everyone has cleared out of the square by now. There are only about twenty or so families left, and a few other stragglers on their way out.

"I bet they'll kill them all as soon as they get out of Woden limits. What use would they have for a truckload or two full of useless children?" The words enter my mind, and I wheel around finding the person to which the words had come from.

Before I know what I am doing I have knocked him to the ground, and end up kneeling above him ready for another shot at him. As he wipes the blood from his lip, I recognize him. Harland, a boy of nineteen. He isn't tall, but he has wide, strong shoulders, and arms that consist almost entirely of muscle. He must outweigh me by at least one hundred pounds. I know my adrenaline is the only thing that allowed me to take him down like I did. My brothers are upon me before Harland can make his move pulling me to my feet and restraining me to keep me from making the mistake of taking another shot at him.

"Ell, what has gotten into you?" Clem says in a tone I've never heard him use before as he holds my face between his hands and Reg grips my arms as tightly as possible.

"You're lucky you have your big brothers here to protect you, otherwise you'd be dead Jadim." Harland spits.

"Go home Harland." Clem says shaking his head.

"He said they're going to kill Koen! He called him useless Clem!!" I scream in a fit of hysterics as I drop to my knees as the brief surge of adrenaline starts to leave my body and I begin to tremble as I kneel there.

Harland finally begins to get up, pushing his long dark hair out of his face he snarls at me, but does not retaliate, and I know he is right that him sparing me was only thanks to my brothers. I'm still sniffling when Reg jerks me to my feet once more and holds me firmly by the arms. His face is hard, and I can tell that he is clenching his jaw, holding onto an even deeper anger.

"Aella you listen to me!" He starts through clenched teeth. "Do you think this is any way to spend the last few minutes you have with Koen, starting fights? Do you know what would have probably happened to you if Clem and I hadn't been here? Harland very well could have killed you if he wanted!" Reg is trying to control his anger, but I can feel his fingers digging into my arms.

"But Reg, he said…" I cry out, but before I can get the words out Reg slaps my face.

"I could care less what he said! Koen is being taken from us, and you go and start a fight! Look at him! The poor kid is over there crying his eyes out! Damn it Aella!!" Reg releases his grip on me and backs away as my father joins us.

Those who remain in the square all have their tearstained faces turned towards us and only then do I realize what a scene we are making. But fortunately the attention does not stay on us long because we all hear the sound of trucks coming down the stone streets towards the east side of the square. Upon hearing this my brothers, father and I rejoin my mother, Koen and Phoibe. I see my mother take my father's hand and squeeze it tight.

I look in the direction of the stage and see that workers are already starting to disassemble it. A little to the right of the stage Damon stands with Cari, their entourage of strangers now nowhere to be found. They appear to be in some sort of argument, for Cari's beautiful features seem to be hardened, and she keeps making significant gestures as if to amplify her words. Damon stands unmoved looking in the direction of the trucks only making a comment every so often, each of his words seem to send Cari into a deeper rage. Finally, Damon, in a single swift motion, moves his hand past Cari's face, and she falls silent and still. My eyes widen at the sight, it was if he had just shut her off. A wicked smile graces Damon's lips as he walks to the center of the square robotically, Cari follows closely behind him. The trucks finally emerge from around a building and wind their way to where Damon stands.

They are military style trucks with canvas covers on the back. On each cover, Nirvana's familiar national emblem is printed, and under it is our ever-present national motto. Our national symbol is a shield divided into four sections. The top left and bottom right sections are black, and the others are white. In the middle of the shield is a diamond that is twisted at the sides. This symbol can be found on almost anything that has been issued by the government including clothing, food wrappings, and any papers we receive.

The drivers of the trucks, dressed in the same black armor as the Allure officers get out and open the doors on the back of the trucks. Guns at the ready they stand by the doors and await further instruction.

"Now then." Damon calls out, his booming voice ringing loud and clear in our ears, "I am going to call out a list of names, when I call the name of your child, parents please bring them forward to be loaded." He begins to list names, and one by one children are loaded into the trucks. I see people I know, people my family knows, friends of Koen's, all with horrified looks on their innocent faces.

Women carrying infants make their way slowly to the back of the trucks, and can barely stand as their babies are taken and handed off to one of the older children that have already been loaded. The sound of crying provides the only noise other than Damon's voice, and I can hardly focus on exactly who is being called until he says the one name I am quietly hoping has somehow been left off the list.

"Koen Jadim."

The sound of his name being called reminds me that I'm awake, this is undoubtedly happening, there is nothing I can do, and I may never see him again. Slowly we walk forward together hand in hand in a rather powerful manor, each give him one more hug as Damon checks his name off the list in his hands and then Koen is taken from us and loaded into the truck.

Seeing Damon up close sends chills down my spine. I knew he was tall, but I didn't expect him to tower over me by a whole foot. I am now able to get a better look and his eyes and only now do I realize that they are lined with black makeup, but that is not the only thing that is unusual. His pupils seem to be stretched vertically making them more oval shaped than round. As I walk past him, I glance at his hands as one of his long boney fingers runs down the list, and finds the next victim to be loaded.

We remain beside the truck a moment, watching as confused looking families that were not present for the meeting make their way into the square. One of the officers soon approaches us to say that we must leave the square, which after a brief moment, and a final look at Koen's sweet face we all do reluctantly. Not a minute after we turn to go do we hear the scream followed closely by a gunshot and several more terror filled shrieks.

4

She clutches her already blood stained chest as the life leaves her body and she falls to the ground. The officer that had taken the shot stands with his gun still aimed at the other families. Her husband falls to his knees at her side screaming through tears, disbelief and pain, all contributing to the distortion of his words. A girl of about thirteen tries to jump from inside one of the trucks in an attempt to reach her mother but is restrained at once. All of the other families and children stand frozen in terror. The only people to move are the husband of the woman now resting in a pool of blood on the ground and Damon, who gestures to the officers, now all standing at the ready, to lower their weapons.

"Let this be a warning then." Damon calls out tightening his jaw, "No one who attempts to defy the orders of King Fino will go unpunished. This woman was trying to get her child back, but I can assure you there is no need, your children will be well looked after. Although I am not at liberty to divulge the exact details of what their stay in Scheol will entail, I will tell you that you have no reason to worry. You can be very sure that special treatment awaits them."

The way he uses the word treatment sets me on edge, and Cari who seems to be back to normal, has a sinister smile that adds to my steadily growing hatred of the two of them. I have no trust or respect for either of them at this point, and from what I can see neither does anyone else, but the fear of death binds us all so we don't dare show it.

"Liar." The man who lost his wife spits out suddenly and begins to rise slowly from the ground, his trembling hands coated in her blood.

"Liar!!" He repeats as his rage drives him forward towards Damon, but about his third step he falls with a bullet in his head, the sound of the gunshot still resounding in our ears.

"Well now you can be with your wife once again." Damon says with a sick laugh. "Is there anyone else who would care to join them? Anyone who would care to challenge the orders of their king? Or dare to say that his word that I bring to you is not word of truth?"

Stale silence fills the air as nobody dares to move, and we all watch two officers retrieve the bloodstained bodies, and carry them away. Their daughter watches in horror as they are taken out of sight, the shock and suddenness of the events leaving her unable to even scream. Damon breaks the silence with a stern command.

"Those of you whose children have already been loaded are required to leave the square, and I suggest you do so quickly. This shocking display of defiance has already put me behind. So, I will need your full cooperation in order to put my associates and me back on schedule. If you don't care to cooperate, I would be more than happy to have my friends here help change your minds."

Instantly several families, including my own, move swiftly from where we have been lingering out of the square. We walk home without a word, the shock of the day's events leaving us speechless. Even Clem, who rarely has nothing to say, walks with his eyes on the ground, lips pulled tightly together, trying his hardest to choke back another wave of tears.

The sound of gunshots and screams continue to plague my mind. Rona was the only person I'd ever seen dead in my whole life, and now I had seen two more all in a matter of minutes, and what makes it all worse is that I watched them die. I get chills as my mind replays over and over the sight of the life leaving their bodies before they could even hit the ground.

The night is a quiet one in our home and none of us in the mood to eat. Clem and I walk straight to our room. Outside the terror drags on as families that did not heed Damon's warnings about refusing to comply are hunted down. Shrieks of destroyed mothers as their beloved children are stripped away from their protective grasp. My heart aches for them as I toss and turn beneath my thin blanket, trying to make myself as small as possible. I move to the side of my cot that is farthest from the window, but the cracks in our old house continue to allow the sound of pain to slip through and invade my mind. Some shouts are distant, others are frighteningly close.

"I didn't think there were so many…." Clem says quietly from where he sits behind me, the first words since we've been home. "Those that are unable to work I mean."

"Me either." I breathe.

"I wish it would stop." Clem groans as another shriek fills the stale air.

"I feel bad for them. I can't imagine what that would do to you. What a horrid last memory of their families."

"More horrid than surrender?" Clem scoffs.

"What?" I ask, rolling over to face him.

"More horrid than what we did? Just giving Koen up like that. We didn't even fight for him! We allowed them take him! We just handed him over to them!"

"You'd rather have him remember us being beaten? Or worse, killed like that poor little girl's parents? You saw her face, she will never forget that."

"I'd rather him remember us as gallant...His older brothers stepping in, and taking whatever blow they had to in order to let him remain here with us."

"You really think anything you did would have changed their minds? You would rather leave him with the memory of his family being killed right in front of him, feeling totally helpless?" I ask harshly, sitting up now. "There is nothing we could have done. I hate it just as much as you do, perhaps more. I'm the one who asked father if Koen and I could come along this time, and if it wasn't for that then maybe we could have run. Maybe we could have gotten him out of here, but it's too late for regret now. What's done is done and as much as we'd all like to change today's events, we've no power to do so."

"We still could have tired." Clem says, hardly listening to me.

"You sound a great deal like Reg right now you know that? You've got his same pigheaded attitude right now, and let me just point out that it's not a flattering trait for anyone."

"Forget I said anything, Aella." Clem snarls, getting up to leave the room, then turning back to me. "Just forget it.

"Clem…" I start, but he shuts the door forcefully behind him. I allow my head to fall back on my cot and close my eyes tight.

The evening drags into the night, and my eyelids finally start to feel heavy, but horror keeps me from sleep. Each time I start to drift off my chest gets tight as the image of Koen watching our family standing there as he is carted off comes into my mind. Soon the torture of trying to sleep becomes too much, so I rise slowly and make my way to the door. I am quiet so that I don't wake Clem or Phoibe who slipped in sometime just after dark.

The thin hallway is dimly lit by the light of the golden-red moon. I do my best to avoid the floorboards that are notoriously loud when treaded upon. Suddenly a hand lands roughly on my shoulder and I am shoved forcefully against the wall.

"Where the hell are you going?" Reg growls at me, his breath tainted with the strong scent of alcohol.

"I just wanted to step out for a minute." I reply, cowering against the wall, and pulling my arms up to cover my face.

"Don't you dare take one bloody step out that door." Reg snaps, pushing my hand away and swinging at me again, catching the side of my face with the back of his rough hand. "Do it and just see what happens Aella. So help me, I will…"

"Reg?" Phoibe's soft voice calls out, catching Reg's attention. "Reg, what are you doing?"

I instantly feel Reg's grip on my shoulder loosen and I slip away from him down the hall a few steps, covering my stinging cheek lightly with my hand.

"Reg, come on to bed." Phoibe whispers, taken back slightly as she approaches him and smells his breath.

"Don't let her leave." Reg points back at me, but allows Phoibe to pull him through the door to our room.

I stay still in the hall a while before moving briskly through the rest of the house and grabbing my shoes on the way out the door. The moon is full and bright golden-red, casting eerie shadows on the tired ground. I hug the walls of the various shops and homes trying to remain unseen. A few people move along in the shadows on the opposite side of the small street, but none of them pay me any notice.

The air is cold on my skin and I enclose my arms around my waist, caving in my shoulders. My feet against the ground make the only noise after a while, as the terrors of the shrieking seems to have come to a close at long last. I glide along the back streets, moving slowly in the dim light. I am unable to control my heart as it flutters at any sound around me, but it is still much better than being at home. My stomach growls at me for neglecting it, but I feel an emptiness that is so much more substantial than hunger, I continue to ignore it. My mind begins to wander off as I walk, wondering what is to become of Koen, and if I will ever see him again.

Suddenly a figure in the distance catches my attention. I pull as close as I can to the nearest wall and stand still. The figure moves quickly which causes me alarm. It ducks in and out from the shadows until it stops finally in an area so dark I can hardly make out its harsh motions back in the direction from which it came. A moment of hesitation follows this movement before a second figure emerges from the dark. This figure is much smaller than the first, and it ducks in behind the first. They begin moving together with impressive speed in my direction. Sinking down against the wall I hold my breath in hopes that I will go unnoticed. I slide my knees up to my chest and wrap my arms around them. The two figures are but yards from me, but appear to set on moving forward to notice me.

Both of them have their hoods up, but now that they are close it is easy to determine that the bigger one is a boy and the smaller one a girl. They are almost directly in front of me when the girl suddenly comes to a screeching halt.

"What is it?" The boy asks, turning around and heading back towards her, his voice sounding muffled as if it were covered with something.

"I can't…" The girl shakes her head, her voice trembling.

"You have to trust that everything is going to be okay." The boy says, placing his hand firmly on her shoulder.

"It's not that…It's just that I can't leave the others." The girl shakes her head again before looking up into the boys face.

"Mai, you know you can't help that. Now we have to hurry, okay kid? If they find us then we're in big trouble, and I can't stand the thought of anything happening to you." He has both hands on her shoulders now, speaking in a soft, soothing voice.

"You know what this means though…" The girl hangs her head.

"Please kid, I don't want to think about that." The boy's voice is pleading now and his face level with hers. "Be strong here. Make me proud huh?"

After a moment the girl nods and allows him to take her hand and continue to lead her, and finally I am able to take in a normal breath as I let my legs fall limp against the dirt. I look after them as they run along, hoping quietly that they would find favor and succeed in whatever plans they have.

With a heart heavier than before, I pick myself up off the ground. So I don't draw any attention in the direction in which they disappeared, I decide on the long way home. The path I take leads me towards the square. I move quickly through it to keep my frail heart from breaking.

Rounding the corner of our small street I look ahead to see someone standing before my father's shop. Frozen once more I stand in the shadows, waiting. It is only a moment before they move away and once they are out of sight I take off and don't stop running until I am safe behind the door of our house. I slip down the hall trying to slow my breathing. I glide through the door to our room as the sound of Reg's snoring spills out into the hall. I look over at him, sprawled over the side of his cot and onto Phoibe's. Phoibe, in turn, has pulled herself into the smallest space she can to accommodate him. Clem has his thin pillow pulled tightly over his head and turns lightly in his sleep. The moonlight spills through the small window reflecting the pattern of the cracked glass on the floor. My heart continues to pound as I fall on my cot, not bothering to pull the covers over me as I have started to sweat. I shut my eyes, and though it takes me a while, I am able to drift off to sleep.

* * * * *

An untouched plate of food sits on the floor next to my cot. I don't remember her coming into the room, but my mother must have brought it.

A knock at a door somewhere else in the house startles me, and soon after I hear the door shut my father's voice rings out, calling everyone to come to the kitchen so we can read the Sun's Day bulletin together. Stepping into the kitchen I notice that my mother, father, Clem and I are the only ones present.

"Where are Phoibe and Reg?" Clem asks sleepily.

"I haven't seen Phoibe this morning, she may have gone for a walk, you know how she likes to, and maybe Reg went with her this time." My mother answers as she pours herself a cup of coffee.

"Candra, I think we should go ahead and start reading, we can fill them in later. A very large order came in this morning, and Aella and I are going to need every minute to work today."

"Alright Elias, I'll read it to them when they come around. Go ahead." She says as she takes a seat, and my father begins to read aloud. The rules, as usual are the first things read, I'm hardly listening, but when he suddenly stops it catches my attention. He surveys the bulletin, and I know he must be at a section that contains new information. My father isn't the best reader, my mother can read much better than him but he still prefers to, being the man of the house. He always flies through the law section because he's read it so many times he practically has it memorized, but whenever he gets to something new he has to read over it at least once before relaying it to the rest of us.

"Elias, would you like some help?" My mother asks quietly as she puts a hand on his arm. As he hands it to her, I see that his eyes are wet with tears.

Skipping the reading of the new laws my mother begins with the next section.

"All those working at small business please take note of your new weekly schedules;

Girls: On Moon's Day and Freya's Day, you will work in the factories. On Woden's Day, you will work in the forest.

Boys: On Moon's Day and Freya's Day, you will work in the forest. On Woden's Day, you will work in the factories.

Boys and Girls: On Sun's Day, Tiu's Day, Thor's Day and Saturn's day, you will work at your family's business.

All other workers, your new schedules are as follows:

Factory Workers; On Sun's Day and Thor's Day, you will work in the forest. On Tiu's Day and Saturn's Day, you will work in the mill.

Mill Workers; On Sun's Day and Thor's Day, you will work in a factory. On Tiu's Day and Saturn's Day, you will work in the forest.

Forest Workers: On Sun's Day and Thor's Day, you will work in the mill. On Tiu's Day and Saturn's Day, you will work in a factory.

Factory, Mill and Forest Workers: On Moon's Day, Woden's Day and Freya's Day, you will report to your regularly scheduled jobs.

Failure to be present at work will result in immediate, severe punishment. New schedule effective as of Moon's Day, tomorrow. Remember, that we are all Working together for the betterment of Nirvana. Work day starts at sunup!" My mother lays the paper on her lap and looks around at each of us, her eyes landing on my father she says, "Oh, Elias."

"Father, how will you ever get all your work done without me?" I cut in as I think over how much I will be gone every week. I worry at the thought of my father having to take on our piles of work single-handed.

"Just as I did before you worked for me." He answers calmly as usual but seeing the apprehension in me, he adds, "I will be fine. Aella, there is nothing to worry about."

"I wonder why they don't have any of the kids coming to work at the mill..." Clem says, lost in his own thoughts.

My father's words are comforting, but I see he is trying to convince himself that it will be okay just as much as he is trying to convince me. He hasn't done as much work as he will have to now in ten years.

"I will have to learn so many new things at my new jobs, and in such little time." I mutter, unsure of myself, and look to my family for reassurance that I can make it though the weeks to come.

"You can do it, Ell. You learn faster than anyone I know." My mother's words are encouraging, and we exchange mild smiles.

Suddenly, the door flies open, and without a word Reg runs through the house towards our room. None of us know quite how to react so we sit and wait to see if he is coming back or not. When he does return, he is panting.

"Have any of you seen Phoibe?" His voice is stricken with panic, and he holds his head in pain.

We all exchange glances and then all together shake our heads no in response.

"Ahg! I can't find her anywhere! I was down by the square when Traesa came up to me and asks me where Phoibe was headed this morning, I told her that I had no idea what she was talking about and as I walked away I didn't think much of it. Traesa is old, and I figured she was most likely mistaken but then I got worried and now I've been looking all over, and I cant seem to find her!"

"I'm sure everything is fine dear." My mother rises and puts her hand on his arm in an attempt at reassuring him.

"Um, I'm sorry to bother you, but I have a message for Reg." Ailish enters the room and removes his hat. "I knocked, but there wasn't any answer. I'm in a bit of a hurry myself, so I let myself in. I hope I'm not disturbing you."

"Oh no, you're alright Ailish. Have a seat?" Clem gestures to an open chair but Ailish refuses.

"Thank you but I've got some business to attend to, I only dropped by to give you this." Ailish responds handing Reg a small folded piece of paper. He then gives a slight nod of the head, puts back on his hat, and leaves.

"Who's that from?" Asks Clem leaning in close to Reg, but before Reg answers he rushes out of the house calling after Ailish.

When he reenters the house he hands the now crumpled note to Clem and runs to the back room. Clem passes the note to me mother who straightens it out and reads.

"My Dearest Reg, I love you so much more than I can say. I want you to know that I am safe, and you needn't worry about me. I promise I won't be gone long. The other day I received a message from my mother in Aject asking me to come there, I must go, and I promise that I wanted to tell you, but I feared you would not let me go alone. Not that I don't want you with me, trust me when I say that I miss you already and wish you were with me now, but I know how hard it would be for you to get out of work even for a day so I just went. I hope I haven't caused you any stress or worry. I also hope that I haven't left you in any sort of danger, after last nights horrors in the city I almost didn't go away for fear they would hunt me down or go after you and the rest of the family, but Reg, my mother needs me and I felt as though I must go. I'm so terribly sorry I didn't tell you! I love you so much. Please don't worry about me! I am not sure when I will be returning home, but I can assure you, it won't be too long! You are always in my heart, Phoibe."

"She left that note with Ailish sometime very early this morning. He said she gave him specific instructions not to give it to me until at least midhour today. I'm going after her." Reg says as he walks back into the kitchen with a small bag in hand.

"Reg you can't! She says she is going to be fine, and she'll be home soon son." My father is attempting to stop Reg as he looks through a box for his knife.

"Father, you know Phoibe couldn't possibly make it all the way to Aject alone. She can hardly make it to the square without getting herself into some sort of trouble. She's so weak father, and she's not the type to take food from us as provisions, family though she is, she wouldn't want to short us even the slightest bit She will think that we need it more that her and try to find things as she goes. She's going to have to go through the Melaine Forest, I have to go after her." Reg shakes his head and starts for the door.

"Reg, listen to Father, you don't even know for sure what path she took. Not only that but she left early this morning. She'll have at least a good nine or ten hours on you by now if not more so there is no possible way you could catch up." Clem tries to reason with him, but Reg simply swings his now full bag onto his back.

"I'll run. I'll steal a motorbike. I'll catch her Clem. I'm not going to lose her. I won't let the loss of another member of this family be on my shoulders." Reg shakes his head as he speaks and his hand trembling at his side.

"Reg, please. We may already be in enough trouble when Phoibe is found missing from work. The bulletin came today and it had specific instructions about being at work, and those who are absent will face serious punishment."

At Clem's words Reg falls into a chair and puts his head in his hands.

"Come on Aella. We have lots of work today, and we are now very far behind. Clem and Reg you should get to work as well." My father instructs us. He knows Reg is hurting but also knows that sitting around and crying isn't going to keep any of us out of trouble.

"She'll be back soon Reg. Don't worry." I say, but I'm so unsure of my words my voice breaks. Knowing I've only made things worse I run quickly out of the house and join my father in the workshop.

5

I arrive at the factory the next morning just before sunrise. Swills of smoke fumes fill my nostrils, the air around the factory is thicker than what I'm used to breathing so it takes a bit of adjusting. Fire is something I've been around my whole life so the smell of smoke is nothing new to me, but I can tell that these are not just wood fires burning at this factory, because a variety of harsh, unfamiliar smells also fills my nose.

Several heavily armed officers stand at the door of the factory, and one of them holds a list to check everyone in. As I reach the front of the small line, he calls out.

"Name?" His sour voice suggests he doesn't want to be here any more than I do.

"Aella Jadim." I say in a voice so small and timid that it's hardly audible.

"Name?" He calls out again, louder this time.

"Aella Jadim!" I answer almost yelling so he is sure to hear me.

He looks at me with his face full of distain then turns back to his list. Finding my name he tells me with an extreme lack of interest since he has probably already given this same speech one too many times this morning.

"Listen very carefully to what I am about to tell you. I will not be repeating this, and if you are not where you are supposed to be then your workday will not be counted. Do you understand me?" I nod, and he continues, "Alright, you are in Section C, you will be making bullets. You enter the building through these doors. Once you are inside, follow the signs to your section. Once in your section go to the third assembly line on the right. You are in the very last seat on the far side of that line."

"Yes sir." As I say this, I walk slowly through the menacingly large doors of the factory.

Reading the signs as I go, I finally make it up several flights of stairs to Section C. Just as the man at the door instructed, I take my seat at the end of the third line. Next to me sits an elderly woman who appears to be no less than about sixty. She is unable to sit up straight, and I can only imagine how many hours she must have spent leaning over the table that lies before us. She smiles with what teeth she has left, and waves one of her gnarled hands at me.

"You must be one of the new folks huh?" She says.

It's unlike me to be so timid, but my voice comes out softly as I answer.

"Yes ma'am."

"I knew I hadn't seen you before. I would have remembered you if I had met ya'. I don't forget faces much, especially those as pretty as yours. I'm Sibylla, what's your name?"

"Aella." This time my voice comes out much more confident than the first time.

"Well that's a beautiful name! And don't be scared dear, it isn't as bad here as it seems. Besides, old Sibylla here will make sure she takes good care of you." She chuckles as she lightly hits my arm.

It isn't hard to see that Sibylla was once a beautiful woman. Although she is worn, her large brown eyes dance as she talks and tell a story of a once tall, confident and beautiful young girl.

"Is it hard?" I ask still in awe of her novelistic eyes.

"Is what hard?"

"Making bullets."

"Oh well this is the first day that we've been required to make them. I used to work on clothes. Our manager told us at work on Sun's Day that we have received special orders straight from Scheol. How hard can it be though? And if an old bat like me can do it then it shouldn't be any problem for you!" She smiles to herself as she positions herself over the table and awaits the box of shells from the woman sitting next to her. I assume the same position and wait to receive them from her.

"Looks like all you have to do is reposition them in the box." Sibylla says shoving the box my way.

"What do you have to do?"

"Nothing too bad, just clip the heads on them." Her hands are shaking so badly as she tries to clip the first shell from the next box on it's pitiful.

"How about we switch jobs? As long as we're both doing something they can't get mad about that can they?" I offer, and relief instantly fills her eyes. She nods her head in thanks, then rises slowly to trade places with me.

About four hours later a static-like noise is heard overhead. We all stop work to listen as an announcement is made about a short break that we will be allowed for lunch. All at once the room erupts with movement as people rise from their stations and head to any open areas where they can eat their lunches. Only now do I realized that everyone working on our floor is a woman, although I saw many men around the factory on my way in that morning. Sibylla and I make our way to a small space in the corner of the large room. I have to help her along since her curved back prevents her from straightening herself into a full standing position. Not long after we get ourselves situated Sibylla points out a short, timid-looking, dark-haired girl standing alone in one of the aisles between assembly lines.

"She looks scared, maybe she would like to come sit with us. What do you think?"

I answer by rising and walking towards the girl. Upon seeing me coming, her already timid face becomes even more so. She is no taller than five feet, and her dark hair flows down her back. She wears a pair of black coveralls that have been cut off just above her knees with a faded blue t-shirt underneath. Her small square glasses are crooked, and one of the lenses has a small crack in it. By her size and innocent face I judge her to be about fourteen at the most.

"Would you like to come sit with us?" I gesture to a seated Sibylla who waves. Instantly her face lights up and she nods, still not saying a word. When we sit I notice she doesn't have a lunch with her so Sibylla and I quickly divide parts of our lunches in order to share. We sit in silence for a while and eat, then for the first time she speaks.

"My name's Liridona. Thank you for sharing with me, nobody has said as much as a word to me since I got here this morning except for the exceptionally grouchy man at the door. Working here is so strange compared to my mother's sewing shop, although it is nice to see more people. I don't get to see many people in the shop, I work in the back and so I hardly know anyone around. I'm sixteen. I know I don't look it, but I am. You both are very kind. What are your names?"

All the words pour out of her mouth so quickly I am surprised that I catch most of them. Her voice is bigger than I had anticipated, and the sudden burst of confidence out of her catches me off guard, and I almost forget to respond.

"I'm Aella, and this is Sibylla." I finally manage, then add, "It's my first day working here too. You sure do talk more than I expected you would."

"I get that a lot. Well, I suppose it's a lot. Almost everyone I talk to says that, not that I meet a lot of people. But that's okay I am quiet at first. I talk lots more once you get to know me. I'm sorry, mother says I talk too much. I suppose I get that from her though. I mean you should hear her talk! She goes on and on, and I am sure everyone who comes in the shop is bothered by how she keeps them, and she just doesn't see that she's doing it, you see so there is really no hope in her stopping. Sorry." She says looking down as she strokes her hair.

"Don't worry about it." I smile.

"My sisters tell me I'm obnoxious, but they aren't much better I think. We're all talkers."

"You said you work for your mother?" I ask, taking a bite of cheese.

"Oh yes, she owns a tailor shop. Have you ever been to the south side of the city? It's near where the market people set up their shops, an ideal location if you ask me. Though it doesn't sound like it would be very important, but lots of things get torn in the various jobs available. Most people don't really know about us though, as good of a location as we have, people just don't come so it's rough. The Sweep makes it even worse. Where did you get that?" Liridona says as I begin to unpack my lunch.

"This?" I ask, holding up a piece of cheese. "My father got it as a portion of pay from someone who came into his shop the other day. He does a good deal of that sort of trade, goods for work. Do you want some?" Not waiting for a response I break off a piece and extend it towards an excited looking Liridona who receives it with a bright smile. "I know what you mean about the ripped clothes though. My older brothers come home all the time with tattered clothes, but they continue to wear them no matter how bad they get, drives my mother crazy. But it isn't like clothes are a top priority around here. My mother would be happy to know about your shop." I say as I look up to find

Liridona turning the cheese over in her small hands. "You ever had cheese before?" I ask.

"No never, but I heard its delightful stuff!" She smiles.

"Well go on and eat it then." I tell her.

"If you don't mind I'd like to take it home with me." Liridona replies timidly. "My family will be happy try it, and I couldn't live with myself if I got to have some and they didn't."

"In that case you better take enough to share." I smile as I dump the rest of my lunch out in front of me. I place the rest of the cheese back inside and pass the bag to Liridona.

"Oh no, I couldn't take this." She protests.

"Really, it's fine. I don't much care for it to being with. It's all yours. Honestly, if I have to have more we've got plenty."

"Thank you." She smiles. "Really, thank you so much."

We continue to talk for the rest of the break. Sibylla listens as Liridona and I exchange stories of working for our parents and slowly discover how alike we are. Liridona's family is worse off than mine though. Although her mother owns her own business they don't get too many customers, and they often end up working on things for free if a family can't afford to pay.

I begin to like Liridona more and more. As she speaks, she uses her hands in large theatrical movements that make Sibylla and I laugh. Our break ends only too quickly, and we hustle back to our stations to continue working. The work seems easier now, and the rest of the day flies by.

Only when I reach home do I begin to feel my back growing stiff. I begin to wonder if I will ever be able to stand up straight again when my mother comes to my rescue and gives me a massage. We talk little about my day at the factory, I only mention a few small details, and although the work wasn't hard I am weary and wish to go straight to bed. I do so briefly after dinner. Lying on my cot, I can't help but smile. The thought of getting to know people makes me so happy, and I can hardly wait for the next chance I get to see Liridona and Sibylla. I fall asleep happy that my first day at the factory was much better than I had previously thought it would be, and the terror of working outside my father's shop slowly begins to diminish.

6

I wake early the next morning, the pain of the past days work taking hold of my muscles as I make my way slowly to the kitchen. My mother sits at the table with a glass of water as my father finishes off a piece of toast.

"Morning." I say as I sit myself down at the table with them.

"Big order today Aella, as soon as your done meet me the in the shop." My father says firmly rising from the table and heading out the door.

Before I can respond, he is gone. I look to my mother for an answer about my father's unusually harsh words.

"He's worried Aella. A great deal of orders came in yesterday when you were away. That wouldn't be so strange if all of them weren't for weapons. There were even some things described that were completely new. He's going crazy trying to get them all done. He was up half the night working on them. I just don't see how they can expect him to do all this work on his own. At least he enjoyed work when you there. Now he has too much time to think. It's not good for a man to think so much."

"Weapons? What kind?" I ask, then recalling my day at the factory I throw out, "You know we made gun shells yesterday, at the factory. Tons and tons of them, my line alone made at least a quarter of a million. One of the women I was working with told me that yesterday was the first day they've been required to make them, that there have been some sort of special orders coming straight from Scheol."

"I spoke to Clem last night. He told me they have had to start building strange wooden structures by the mill. Then Reg said that work in the forest yesterday seemed more like combat training for men, and women were sent to gather a much larger sum of food than normal. Who knows though, perhaps the Scheol officials are simply attempting to prepare us for winter?" My mother shrugs and goes to put the dishes in the sink, but her last statement seems a little far-fetched.

Winter? What possible way would guns be helping us in preparation for winter? Besides, winter is months away. I ponder over possible scenarios for our sudden increase in demand for military supplies while I work diligently in the shop. I have heard of war before, sometimes our teachers in school would refer to The Attack as the Great War. But, considering the fact that the entire world was destroyed with the exception of my people I can't seem to find any possible opponent for us to wage war against.

By the end of the day, I conclude that the Allure must be expecting to have a harsh winter and want to be as prepared as possible, even if some of the things we have been asked to create don't quite fit the theory it is the most reasonable thing I come up with.

* * * * *

Woden's Day morning seems to come all too soon. Slightly before sunrise Reg and I begin the three long walk to the forest, which sits against the south line of the city limits. We exchange few words as we walk, and I can tell that Reg is growing more and more anxious about Phoibe. In her letter, she said that she wouldn't be gone too long, but "too long" could mean just about anything, and with each passing day, Phoibe's empty cot seems more and more ominous.

When we finally reach the woods Reg speaks.

"I'll try my best to get you assigned to my hunting group so that I can look after you. Wait here."

His words "so that I can look after you" only confirm my thoughts of how anxious he is becoming. I rub my foot across the dirt creating a small indention, the thought of Reg being so anxious concerns me, the possibility of him running away in search of Phoibe growing more probable. After a few minutes Reg returns so where I am waiting.

"Come on." Reg says as he rejoins me, then heads briskly towards a small shed that sits just inside the tree line.

"Wait." He commands me as we reach our destination, pointing to the spot where he wishes me to stand until he comes back.

I feel much like a small child being told what to do in such a manner, but regardless, I wait. Suddenly I hear shouts from inside the shed, Reg's voice is among them. I rush to the door just as it flies open, and Reg stumbles out followed closely by a man who is much bigger than him. The man has hair the color of gold and walks in an exceptionally arrogant manner. As he strides out the door, I identify the shinny object he is holding, a knife.

"Reg!!" I scream as my brother, who has his back to the man, attempts to return to his feet. Shocked, I stand unsure of myself as though fear has glued me to the ground, then just as Reg makes it up and turns around a boy darts out of the woods stopping himself in the path of Reg's attacker, causing the man to stop short.

"Pathetic Reg. If it wasn't for this teenager, you would be dead right now." The man's gruff voice is loud and powerful. He takes a quick look at me before walking into to forest.

"Reg, are you okay?" The boy asks, looking over Reg for any injury.

"I'm fine Aeton, thanks." Reg responds as he straightens up.

"Are you alright?" I still haven't moved when the boy starts to speak to me.

"I'm fine." I say quietly before rushing to Reg and throwing my arms around him. "Who was that?" I ask as I look towards the forest into which Reg's attacker had disappeared.

"Orfeo." Reg's voice is filled with an emotion that is beyond hatred. "Not anyone worth getting to know."

When Reg speaks the name, I am instantly taken back to the night Reg was so drunk and poured so many things out to me. I recall his saying that he was surprised that Phoibe didn't leave him for a man named Orfeo, and I also remember him holding up his right arm and telling me what Orfeo had been the one responsible for the loss of his hand. Reg had called what happened to his hand an accident when it had initially happened. But now I am able to see that although he had been wronged he protected Orfeo by saying nobody was at fault for what happened. Reg is not one to fight when it is not necessary, so he lied in order to avoid another fight.

"What happened? I say, staring at Reg.

"I went in to get my pack and Orfeo was sitting at the table sharpening his knife, he made a comment about Phoibe. He said that he heard she left me and wasn't coming back. I told him that I would appreciate him staying out of my business and wouldn't get involved in Phoibe's affairs. He responded like a grown up by getting up and throwing me out the door."

"Oh Reg, I'm so sorry, he could have killed you, and I just stood there!" My arms wrap around my brother once again as I speak, then I turn and find the boy who had saved him.

"If it hadn't been for you, I…well, thank you." My words come out broken and not at all like I plan for them too.

"No problem. Oh and uh I'm sorry about the other day in town." He says as sincerity floods his eyes.

At first I am confused, but as I take a closer look at his face, it hits me. He was the boy who ran into me in the square a few days back. His face is not one that I would let myself easily forget. He has stunning blue eyes that beckon you into them, small hints of gold grace the center of them just around the pupil, as I look up at him, I can't help but stare into them. Those incredible eyes hide behind a pair of thin-rimmed, square glasses. His hair is light brown, but it also has small highlights of golden blonde. It is not terribly long, and it sticks up in various places. His jaw line and chin are both well defined and make him appear much more like a man rather than a teenager. He wears a t-shirt, that he has cut the sleeves off of, revealing his muscular arms. I can't quite tell what it is, but something about him causes my heart to race. I find it hard to take my eyes off him. A cute crooked smile forms on his lips and I realize I must have been staring for longer than I thought.

"Don't worry about it." I say at long last, one look from Reg confirms my suspicious that I had been making a fool of myself by staring.

"Aella, this is Aeton. Aeton, my sister, Aella." Reg says as he looks back and forth between he two of us. "Aeton is in our hunting group as well."

"You'll be joining us?" Aeton looks to me.

"Looks like it." I smile. His voice is deep and has a sort of rhythmic quality to it that makes me long to get him engaged in a longer conversation just to hear him talk.

The day consists of rigorous training with different weapons. I learn remarkably quickly that I am not, by any stretch of the imagination, good with a bow and arrow. Although Reg and Aeton assure me that I will get the hang of it, I have some serious doubts. I am the best with a sword, and by the end of the day I am able to give

Reg a real run for his money, but part of me still thinks he was going easy on me.

The more time I spend around Aeton, the fonder I grow of him. He is patient and understanding. His ability to throw a knife is unlike anything I have ever seen. Even Reg's abilities seem mediocre at best in comparison. He tries to teach me, but I'm hardly decent at it.

I pick up the knife, and he points out a target for me, a tree, not ten feet from where I stand, and I miss, badly. Aeton bites his lip to keep from laughing, and quickly goes to retrieve the knife, to hide his amused expression.

"Sorry." I say with a slight smile taking the knife from his outstretched hand. I glance up as I draw the knife back and my eyes become glued to his.

"You'll get the hang of it. Here, let me show you." Without taking his eyes off mine, he moves around behind me. "Now," he says lifting my right hand that holds the point of the knife up to my shoulder. "Make sure you have a good grip on the handle. Got it?"

"Got it." I answer as I continue to look over my shoulder at him.

"Good, now just look at your target, and remember you are going to be using your wrist, and just throw." I turn just as he instructs me. His hand still on mine, I throw the knife again, this time sticking it in the tree. Looking at me with approval Aeton says. "Look now, I told you that you'd get the hang of it." He says as his cute crooked smile finds it's way back onto his face.

"That only worked because you practically threw it for me." I blush.

"Oh no, that was all you. Here, give it another go." Aeton hands me another knife before taking a drastic step backwards.

I look at him, uncertain, but eventually I throw it, and it is no surprise when I miss.

"See! I told you, I couldn't do it myself." I say, slightly embarrassed.

"Oh I know, you were nowhere close! I just wanted to see you try again. You're bloody awful." Aeton says as he leans against a tree.

I try my hardest to seem offended, but I can't help but laugh along with him. For the rest of the day, Aeton continues to make jokes about my lack of skill, and after a while Reg joins in. I continue to assure both of them that I will practice and soon enough be able to teach both of them a thing or two, but that only makes them laugh harder.

"Aella, I know you, there is no way you are going to practice this." Reg says playfully.

"That's what you think!" I respond, knowing he's right.

"I say you just face facts now, Aella. You will never be any good." Aeton laughs.

"Thank you for the encouragement Aeton, really it means so much to have such an encouraging teacher." I reply, rolling my eyes.

"Anything I can do to help." He smiles.

"Aeton, would you like to join our family for supper?" Reg asks as he winks at me.

"I'd love to! Are you sure that would be okay?" Aeton asks.

"Oh, I'm sure our mother won't mind. She is actually rather fond of the company, though we don't have the pleasure of it very often." Reg answers.

"It wasn't your mother I was worried about, it's this one." Aeton points to me.

"This one?" I say, shoving him.

"Well I guess I should have said, is it safe, rather. I mean if there are going to be any knives at the table I don't want to be anywhere near you." Aeton smiles, clearly satisfied with himself, before shoving me back.

"Oh ha ha. Very funny." I turn away to conceal my smile.

"Yeah, I thought it was." Aeton laughs.

"Well fine, if I promise not to throw anything, would you really like to join us?" I say with a grin.

"I would like that a lot." Aeton winks as me, and I can't help but blush.

7

The next six weeks go on pretty much the same. We still don't know the motive behind all the extra work, and the weekly bulletin fails to shed any light on the subject. So we are forced to press without asking too many questions about any of it. For a time, there was discussion of whether or not the children that were taken would ever be brought back, but after a while the hope of such a thing faded away.

I try my best to keep my mind off of Koen, and being away from my home and family helps me to do so. That is why I look forward to my days at the factory, although the work tends to get boring, I do enjoy getting to see my friends. Liridona and I grow closer each day. It is pleasant to be able to talk to her about Aeton, since the mere thought of him tends to bring a large bright smile to my face.

"So you fancy him quite a bit then, huh? What's he like?" Liridona had asked one day.

"Well, he's tall and handsome, and very kind and patient. He's quite funny too. Oh and he has the most mesmerizing eyes you've ever seen!" I told her excitedly.

"I would rather like to meet him." She winked at me.

"He'll be over for dinner tomorrow, you should join us." I smiled.

"Well I just might do that!" Liridona laughed.

The next night she was at the house for dinner, and she kept saying how jealous she was. The more I get to know her the more I enjoy being around her, and I realize just how ridiculous she is.

Sibylla too, never fails to make me laugh day after day, but she also has her serious moments. She tells me her thoughts on the changes in the rejoin, and she says that she often wonders if the same changes are being made in Aject, something I hadn't seriously considered. After she said that though, she changed her tone quickly.

"Aella, you are going to do great things. Remember that. You have the power inside of you." She whispered.

"That's what my father always tells me, see he gave me this ring and told me, I am the key to my future." I responded lightly, but Sibylla then took firm hold of my wrists and pulled me close so she could speak right into my ear.

"You will be like a whirlwind. You will change things. You will be great. Don't let them deceive you. Stay strong. Nirvana is changing Aella Jadim, and what is to come may surprise you, it may frighten you, it will come close to breaking you, it will try to take you, but remember that you are destined for greatness, not destruction. Find him and find the answer."

"What do you mean?" I had asked, but she refused to answer, and then quickly changed the subject.

I spent the rest of the day in silence, thinking over her words, but I was still lost as I walked home that night. I intended on getting some of my questions answered the next time I saw her, but he next day Ailish showed up at our door to inform us that she had gone missing, which only added to my fear and confusion. I tried my best to keep my mind off of it after that, but my next day at the factory was dull without her and I couldn't stop wondering about her.

Aeton and I also grow closer, I have been taught so much about working in the forest, and I have increased my knife throwing ability by at least one hundred percent, but that truly isn't saying much. I explained everything that had happened with Sibylla to him one day, and he had assured me that it was nothing to worry about.

It doesn't take me long to realize that Aeton speaks exceptionally little of his family. His presence at our home become more frequent, and many times I'd hoped that he would switch things up and invite me to meet his own family, but they all remain a mystery. My parents love to have him over, and he never comes without bringing something small to add to the table when we eat. Not once does either of my parents ask me how I feel about Aeton. I assume they don't think I see him as anything but a friend, and I am okay with that. I am sure my father would try his very best to mess with us if he knew.

Reg seems to notice my fascination with Aeton, but he doesn't say anything about it to me. Occasionally he makes faces at me though after I've finished a conversation with Aeton, and I always blush.

I do though, talk to Clem about him. He pokes fun at me as we talk, but also encourages me some. We talk almost every night before we go to sleep, he tells me about work at the mill, and all the different contraptions they have been constructing lately.

"You really should see these things Aella! They are so strange, and they're huge! We have asked some of the new officers what they're for, but they won't tell us. About half of the men have been instructed to start moving them down towards the shore. It takes a great number of men to transport just one of them, and it is quite the journey down there. Those of us who stay at the mill then end up with double the work and not one of us knows what it is that we're really doing. Nirvana is changing Ell, I can feel it." Clem told me one night after a particularly long day at work, and his last few words have stuck in my mind ever since.

Reg still worries about Phoibe and spend the evenings at Ailish's house waiting to see if Phoibe has written him, but each night returns home empty-handed. He has fallen into a sort of depressed state. He neglects to eat most nights, and I have woken up several times and seen him crying as he reads over the note Phoibe left again and again. We have all tried to stay off the topic whenever we can, and avoid bringing up things that could remind him of her. I know that my new relationship with Aeton must be hard on him, and I figure that is why he generally avoids having conversations about it with me.

Nobody seems to have noticed Phoibe's absence at work though, which comes as a relief. We all worry though that perhaps she never made it though to Aject, but whenever he does bring her up we continue to encourage Reg as much as possible, assuring him that she is in good health, and has been too busy helping her mother to write, or that she has written, and it's just taking some time for the letters to get here. My mother even suggests that her letter got lost, and she is awaiting a reply from him. He tries to write her, but his attempts normally result in an inability to finish.

Other than the occasional new thing I have to learn, things have fallen into a weekly sort of rhythm. Work at my father's shop has not slowed down even the slightest bit, and every time we get an order done several more seem quickly to take its place. The nights after I have been working in the shop I sleep the hardest. Work there takes more out of me than either of my other jobs. I can only imagine how my father must fee when he works there alone. When the new laws first came out, I was devastated about leaving my father's side, but as time has gone on, things have changed in the shop. When I am there my father and I hardly talk as we used to. Even at home my father seems to have fallen silent. I know my mother worries, but she tries not to show it too much. She only tried to talk to him about it once, but it resulted in one of the only fights I had ever seen my parents get into.

"Don't worry Aella, you're father is just worn out." My mother had tried to assure me, I could tell that there was something more, but I chose not to ask.

After about a week, Aeton began to walk with Reg and me to work every Woden's Day, and today is no different. He stands smiling by the front door of my father's shop as we walk out of the house just like so many days before. We make our way to the forest taking our time as we talk along the way. As we turn the last corner of our walk, we see all the forest workers gathered just in front of where the tree line starts. When we get closer, we are able to see that fear covers many of their faces.

"What's going on?" Reg asks as we reach the crowd. A man whom I've never seen before comes to explain.

"Early this morning, a good while before sunup, a group of hunters were making the round, they went a little further out this time since we've almost picked the closer area clean of any resources, just to see what they could find. They were close to the road that runs between Woden and the small southern portion of Aject when they smelled it, the smell of rotting flesh. They followed the smell across the road just into the Melaine Forest, and that's when the carcass was found. The men ran straight back her, and now chief says we are all heading over to check it out."

I have so many questions, but we are told to get our weapons and head out, following the lead of the men who originally found the "creature" as everyone calls it. The walk seems to take forever, and workers are constantly throwing questions out at the group of leaders. The answers given are vague considering how little time they spent looking over the thing before they came running back. Reg's face is virtually expressionless the whole way there, and I know that the thought of the forest does not bring pleasant thoughts to his mind.

There is no mistaking when we are close. The smell of blood and decaying flesh enters my nostrils in a split second and grows increasingly more pungent as we get closer still. It grows so strong that many of us have pulled our shirts over our noses to try and dilute the stench. We have only just crossed timidly over the road and into the Melaine Forest when the body comes into view.

It lies on its side, mouth open wide. Hundreds of flies swarm around it. It looks like nothing I have even seen before in my life. We pour into the break in trees where the carcass is and form a circle around it, each of our faces shows the puzzlement caused by what lies before us. It has the body of some sort of bear although it is much bigger than any I've ever seen or heard of; at least five times the size. Its gaping mouth reveals a set of snakelike fangs. The majority of it is covered in thick brown hair, but there are portions around the beast's paws that are covered in scales. Each paw is roughly two feet in diameter with five razor sharp claws on each of them that extend several inches. The mouth of the beast is not the only thing that is gaping. Its chest has a large hole in it; the flesh around the edges of the hole savagely torn and the nearby fur is coated in an incredibly thick layer of dried blood. It appears as though this creature has had its heart ripped from its chest. Its eyes are gone, having been pecked out by birds by the looks of it. Other portions of its flesh are torn as well, and part of its massive back has caved in allowing a few of its ribs to be visible, each of which is about as thick as my arm.

I turn to comment on the creature to Aeton, only to find that I've lost him somehow in the crowd. Reg is still by my side and looks upon what lies before us with astonishment. Men and women exchange their thoughts about the possible species of the creature. Some even dare to touch it, only to rear back and exclaim how cold its body is, so much so that is almost burns. Others are not able to stand the smell and after throwing up have to move back over to the other side of the road to escape the smell the best they can.

"What do you think it is?" The sound of Aeton's voice behind me breaks my focus on the beast.

"Where did you go? I thought I'd lost you somewhere."

"I wanted to look for its heart. And don't you worry about losing me Aella, in case you haven't noticed I can take care of myself thank you very much." He puts his arm around me and pulls me close, his words are playful, but I sense some other masked emotion in him.

"You want to help me find it?" He asks after a moment.

"Find what?" I ask through the fabric of my shirt that covers my mouth.

"The heart, Aella!" Aeton says excitedly.

"You've got to be joking!" I say pulling myself away from him.

"Not even a little bit." Upon saying this, he grabs my arm and pulls me along with him to the surrounding woods.

"This is disgusting!" I protest.

"So is this smell! Gah, makes a person sick doesn't it. I don't think this is going to come off our clothes. Everyone in Woden is going to be able to smell us from miles away." Aeton laughs to himself.

"I'm glad you think this is so funny." I look at him with a sense of amazement.

"Lighten up would you." He smiles at me.

"I don't see how you aren't the slightest bit concerned about what we just found."

"It's dead isn't it?"

"Well, yes. But…" I start.

"But nothing then. If its dead then I'd say we've nothing to worry about, wouldn't you agree?"

"No I would not agree. If there is one of them, then there very well could be plenty more of them out there! You do realize this is the Melaine Forest, nothing but horrible stories have been told about this place." I say, moving closer to Aeton's side.

"Don't worry, the sun is up now, you know all the scary things that live in here have to go back into hiding when the sun comes up." Aeton jokes.

"Why on earth would you say something like that?" I scowl, and Aeton takes my hand in his trying to be comforting, but it does little to help, and I move even closer to his side.

We walk for a while, making our way outward while traveling in circles around where the body is. When we are about fifty yards from where the other hunters stand Aeton stops me abruptly.

"Aella, look the real reason I needed you to come away from the others is that when I disappeared earlier I found this." Holding out his hand, he reveals a small silver ring with a blue jewel in the middle.

"I've seen this ring before; it belongs to Phoibe. But….no. No, that can't be hers. Aeton, what if that thing…." My voice trails off as I picture the unbearable.

"You told me that she was traveling to Aject didn't you? That means she could have dropped it on her way."

"She has had that ring as long as I can remember. It's one of her most prized possessions, she has never taken it off in all the time I have known her. I think she would notice if it just fell off."

"Well, just try and think positive. I'm sure she's perfectly safe, and besides, if she was moving fast she could have just not noticed it was gone." Although he tries to reassure me, Aeton's words have little effect on my racing heart. I start to put the ring in my pocket, but then change my mind, and hold it out to Aeton.

"Take it, keep it safe. I can't risk taking it home with me and having Reg find it." He nods in understanding and pockets the ring.

"Let's get back." With his arm around me, Aeton and I make our way back towards the others.

* * * * *

The walk back to town seems to take even longer than the walk out did. The fact that I don't generally keep secrets from Reg makes it difficult to talk to him. Every few minutes the temptation to tell him about the ring grows stronger, but I restrain myself. The knowledge that telling him will probably send him into a frenzy, and that it very well could be the thing that would drive him to go finally after Phoibe keeps me from spilling.

We make our way out of the forest just after midhour. Expecting to be forced into finishing out the workday we all begin to prepare ourselves for our various jobs when an announcement is made. The forest work overseer calls out to us as soon as we have all gathered outside of the trees. His voice is crisp and clear as we all stop talking to listen.

"You will be released early today in order to attend a mandatory region meeting tonight in the square. Go home, wash up and I will see you tonight!"

People begin to disperse as soon as he finishes talking, not bothering to ask questions. Aeton walks only part of the way home with us before heading off his own way towards his house just after assuring me that we will see one another tonight at the meeting. When we get home, my mother is ready as usual to make us look more presentable. Clem and my father show up not long after Reg and I. Just as my mother finishes helping us all get in and out of our small single shower quickly and making sure we have on fresh clothes, we hear the sound of the bell summoning us to the center of the town.

Talking about each of our days as we walk, my family and I make our way down the narrow streets all the way to the square. Almost everyone else in the town has already made it there by the time we arrive, the hum of all of their voices making it almost impossible to hear causing everyone to lean and talk louder, only adding to the noise. The scene is so much different from the last city meeting that we had, as everyone in town has made a point of showing up, and doing so on time as not to miss anything. I survey the large crowd in search of Aeton, but as I look around my eyes fall across the thin, menacing face of someone else, his red tattoo extenuated by the late day sun.

8

The sight of Damon standing once more on the stage in the center of the square brings up so many different emotions in me that I can hardly think. As my family and I take our place facing the stage, Damon makes his way to the podium. His entourage of spectacularly dressed companions stands where they did on their first visit on the back of the stage. There is not a noise coming from the people by the time he makes it there, we stand, our hard faces on him as we await the new terror he is sure to bring. He begins speaking with virtually the same few sentences he used the last time we saw him.

"As I'm sure you all now know, my name is Damon. I am Enlightener, and I bring you news from the palace at Scheol." He pauses awaiting a reaction, but we remain unmoved, so he continues, "Today I do not bring you news of a law change, the words I have been sent to relay are much more weighty than that. Citizens of Woden, It is my unfortunate duty to inform you of a great rebellion in the Aject region. Innocent people are dying each day at the hand of your neighbors. We have been monitoring the situation for a while.

The special orders you have been working on for the past few weeks were sent out as a precaution in case something like this were to start, and now it has. So, people of Woden I am here today to inform you that King Fino has been forced to make an unprecedented decision. Nirvana will go to war."

War. The word rings in my ears as Damon continues.

"You are being asked to fight in order to save our nation. All those from the age of fifteen to forty will be required to fight, and any men over forty that we see fit will be required to fight as well. Officers will be coming around tonight to make assessments of families and take down the names of those who will be fighting, and will be handing out instructions for each of you to follow. These instructions will also have your assigned regiment number on them. As for those of you who shall not be fighting, you will pick up the work of those who will be leaving. You can expect to see the list of job that will be open in this Sun's Day bulletin. That is all, you are dismissed to your homes."

All around the square jaws drop at the news, the idea of war makes all of us incredibly uneasy. Every family, including mine, takes hold of one another as those who will stay that the ones who will leave will be safe, and those who are to leave muster as much strength as possible to assure their loved ones that they will be fine.

It takes me a moment to recognize that there was something different about the end of the speech Damon just gave, he didn't conclude with the familiar national motto. It only takes me a moment to realize that he didn't say it because all of Nirvana will not be working together this time. It will be families set against families and neighbors against neighbors.

Tears have found their way into my eyes as I stand facing my family. My mother will be the only one left at home. We all know she will constantly be checking for news of the war to make sure that we are all oaky. The thought of my mother standing outside Ailish's office day after day for any word of hope breaks my heart. All four of us are worried about her, but she instantly begins telling us over and over that she will manage, and she knows that none of us will get hurt. I wish so strongly that her words would be able to convince me of the same.

People are beginning to disperse when I remember Aeton and how he had promised to see me at the meeting tonight.

"I'll meet you at home." I tell Clem, but he takes hold of my arm as I turn away.

"No, come on Ell. If he doesn't find you here, he will come to the house, if he isn't already there." Reluctantly I let him pull me towards home, knowing that my mother would have been worried sick about me.

Suddenly a series of shouts fill the air behind us, and we turn to see a large group of people standing before the stage pointing harshly at those that still stand on it. The mayor cowers behind his two guards, making him seem so much like a child I can hardly stand it. My family stops and watches as people become more and more enraged.

"Where are our children?" Demands a large man, and he receives an echo of his shout from the rest of the group.

"What have you done with them? It's been weeks!" Another woman yells sourly.

"You said we had nothing to worry about but we haven't received so much as a single word about the condition of our children!" The shouts continue.

"You take everyone on home Reg, make sure they get there safely. I'm going to stay here and see what answer that monster gives to that." My father says, pushing Reg towards the rest of us.

"Father…" Reg starts.

"Elias…" My mother says helplessly at the same time as Reg.

"I can get mother and Aella home father, that way Reg can stay here with you in case something were to happen." Clem offers.

"Reginald when I tell you to do something I expect you to do it without so much as the slightest form of hesitation. Take you mother, Clem and Aella and go home now." My father says in a unusually severe tone.

"Yes father." Reg responds, his eyes locked on my fathers.

As my mother, brothers and I walk home I turn the thought of a war over and over in my mind. I will have to fight, and so will Clem, my father and Reg. Reg is the one who worries me the most, although he has mastered the use of a sword he hasn't had anywhere to seriously use it. The thing that helped him keep his job was not so much that he proved he could still do something, but the fact that he was such a wise and skilled teacher. Teaching others is what he has spent most of his time doing since the incident. I shudder at the thought of him in battle.

* * * * *

Clem was right about Aeton, for when we round the corner there he stands, leaning against the door to my father's shop. Seeing him only adds to my fear of the war because he too will be forced to fight in it. My heart pounds as anxiety begins to grow inside of me. I rush to Aeton and throw my arms around him. I hold him tightly for a moment and then release my grip enough to where I can see his face.

"Don't worry Aella, everything is going to be fine. I bet we'll even end up in the same regiment." He says, looking into my eyes.

I try my best to take his words to heart, but although I cant seem to find even the slightest hint of falsity in his voice, I am still unable to fully believe him, but I nod my head as though I do.

"Hello, Aeton." My mother says with a slight smile as she joins us. "You two should come inside, it looks like a storm."

She is right, for when we look up we realize that the sky has grown dark, and, for the first time, I notice the strong wind. We hustle into the house to find Reg and Clem already seated at the table. The dark sky has caused the inside of the house to fall prey to an array of ominous shadows. My mother soon begins to light a series of candles.

"Where is your father?" Aeton asks cautiously.

"He stayed to see what response Damon had to questions about the children that he took last time. He wouldn't let us stay." I answer, running my finger over a crack in the table.

Time seems to be moving slower than it ever has as we all sit around the table and watch the candles slowly become shorter and shorter. Thunder rumbles through the air, and through the window we can see a yellow, orange haze hanging over the street. The sound of the first few raindrops makes my mother even more uneasy, and she soon gets up to pace, and just when it seems as though she is about to go out into the rain and look for him, my father comes through the door.

"Oh Elias, I was worried sick about you." My mother sighs holding him close. "You're soaking."

"It is raining Candra." My father replies, sitting down to remove his dripping shoes.

As we sit my father turns to Aeton, and a look of confusion crossed his stern face.

"You know you are always welcome here Aeton, but won't your parents or siblings be wanting to see you, considering the circumstances?"

"My parents are dead sir, and my little sister, Maiara, was taken away along with the other children the last time Damon came. I have been living alone for a while now, sir."

His words catch me off guard, the vague nature in which he spoke of his family now making sense.

"Oh. I am so terribly sorry, I had no idea. Oh Aeton please forgive me." My father's words come out in pieces, and I can see how deeply he hurts for Aeton.

"That's okay, sir. You couldn't have known. It was an innocent question." Although what I can see of his eyes show pain, his voice sounds as though he has been able to come to terms with his circumstances.

I take his hand in mine and squeeze it tight in order to comfort him a little. He turns his face towards mine and moves his hand so that our fingers are interlocked.

The silence that follows Aeton's words is broken shortly after it starts by a clap of thunder that causes each one of us to jump and me to tighten my grip on Aeton's hand. As soon as the sound of the thunder begins to roll out, our faces all at once become illuminated by lightening. The wind has also begun to pick up, whistling through the cracks in the house and bringing a chill along with it.

"What happened back in the square father?" Clem asks after a long silence.

"He had no answer for those poor people. He responded by sending those big Allure officers out on them to shut them up. Shows a lot about the sincerity of his words before about them being safe. Ten or twelve people got killed in the mix." My father hangs his head.

"Elias, you could have been one of them!" My mother cries.

"I wasn't anywhere close. I stayed close to the edge of the square in case something like that did happen. I figured it would, those men are sick, and now they expect us to all go risk our lives so that they can continue their reign of terror over all of Nirvana." My father slams his fist down on the table as he finishes. A large roll of thunder that shakes the house follows the sound of his fist making us all jump once more.

My mother suggests we move to the room Reg, Clem, Phoibe, and I share since it is in the center of the house. We make our way there using candles to guide us as the storm continues to rage on outside, now introducing an even heavier rain to the mix.

My mother sits on my cot with me and wraps her arms tightly around me. Clem sits with my father, and Reg sits on his own cot.

"Phoibe!!" Reg calls out just as Aeton is about to take a seat on Phoibe's cot.

"What about Phoibe?" My father asks.

"They are coming around tonight to take down a list of all those that will be fighting in the war," Reg's words are rushed, and his voice is overflowing with panic. "When they come here they will realize she's gone and then we'll all be in trouble!"

As he finishes speaking we all start to understand his panic, but before we can respond we hear a banging at the door and a series of shouts distorted by the storm. My father makes his way quickly to the door and returns not too much later followed by four Allure officials. They all survey the room, scrutinizing each of our faces as they do.

"My list says there should be four from this house. Three under forty and the father looks well enough." One of the officers that has positioned himself closer to the door says as he looks over a paper in his hands. "The mother stays."

I am shocked at the officer's words. Only four of us? Phoibe is under forty and should be on the list, but at the same time I feel relief.

"Name?" The man in the front says pointing to Clem.

"Clem Jadim."

"Name?" He says pointing to my father as another officer scrawls Clem's name down on his list.

"Elias."

"Name?" The man asks now pointing to me.

"Aella."

His attention moves to Reg, and again he asks in the same apathetic tone,

"Name?"

"Reg."

We all hold our breath as the man turns and catches sight of Aeton.

"I thought you said four from this house?" He says with a great sense of annoyance.

"That's what the list says." The man answers in somewhat of a panic, and it is obvious he fears his leader.

"You are a member of this family?" The man has now turned his attention back to Aeton.

"I am." Aeton replies without so much as a hint of apprehension but still, I close my eyes out of fear.

"Very well. Name?"

"Aeton."

"Very well here are your instruction lists. We will show ourselves out." The officer's leader says plainly. I open my eyes to realize everyone is just as surprised as I am that no one was aware of the line.

"What will happen when they reach your home Aeton?" Reg asks as we hear the faint sound of our front door shutting. There is nothing that could have prepared me for Aeton's response.

"Nothing I suppose. They won't have reason to go there anyway. As far as the Allure is concerned, I'm nobody because I'm supposed to be dead."

We all sit looking at Aeton expectantly, and he sits on Phoibe's cot looking back at us. This is the second new thing about Aeton that has been divulged in the past hour, and I am beginning to feel like I don't know him as well as I thought.

"What do you mean you're supposed to be dead?" I ask over the every growing sound of thunder.

Aeton hesitates. He looks at me somewhat apologetically and then, knowing he can't simply keep from telling us, reluctantly begins to speak.

"My family and I used to live in Aject. One day my parents were walking home from the factory where they worked when an Allure officer started to harass my mother, it resulted in a fight between him and my father. Fighting for his life my father ended up pulling the man's gun and killing him." He takes a long pained pause before going on. "Pretty soon more officers showed up, my father was strong, but no match for four highly trained officers. My mother was restrained and held there to watch as they beat him to death in the street. Then they forced my mother to lead them back to our house where my sister and I were. When the officers came in, they practically destroyed our house, throwing things and slinging my mother around as they went. Phoibe did her best to protect my sister and me but…"

Phoibe?" Reg cuts in. "My Phoibe?"

"Yes. She lived not far from us and would care for us after she got off of work until my parents made it home. She was trying her best to protect us that day, it was hard work for a twelve-year old girl, but the moment the officers broke through the door to our room she did something with her hands. It knocked the three of us to the ground, my mother screamed, and when the officers came over to us, they said they were sure that we were all dead, but I saw and heard the whole thing as though there was some sort of peculiar force causing them to think we weren't alive. I couldn't move either, as hard as I tried. They left us there, dragging my screaming mother away with them. After a while, I was able to start moving again, and Phoibe was at my side in an instant helping me up, telling me that we had to go. Then she went and grabbed my sister Maiara in her arms and started out the door. I followed her but stopped short when I began to smell smoke. They had lit our house on fire. Phoibe told me to stand back, lifted one of her hands and created a hole in the back wall of the room. She had me crawl through it, and she followed close behind me with Maiara, and then we ran. We didn't stop running or look back until we were well on the other side of town. Smoke had begun to swell in a dark cloud high up in the air when we finally turned around to look. After that we didn't look back again. We continued moving on through the night and for several more days until we reached Woden. The whole time we ran Phoibe said nothing but "Keep Going". Once we were safe in Woden, Phoibe told us that she was going to have to leave us. And she did, at a home where a woman named Sibylla lived. We never had any answers about that night at the house. I didn't hear anything of Phoibe for years, not until the day I starting working in the forest and met Reg. You have no idea how happy it made me to hear that she was healthy. Sibylla took excellent care of us. She didn't let us out much though. Even though the Allure thought we were dead, we couldn't risk giving ourselves away. When I was fifteen, she told us it was time for us to be on our own. Until Damon showed up, Mai and I had been living in an abandoned house behind one of the southern mills."

As Aeton finishes speaking, none of us are sure how to react. We have questions that's for sure but aren't certain where to begin, then suddenly I am able to put something together in my mind.

"It was you." I look at Aeton with an astonished look.

"What was me?" Aeton looks back at me puzzled.

"I saw you the night they took them. You and your sister were running along in an alley, I saw you." I answer.

"Aella, what were you doing out that night?" My mother gasps and Reg looks at me with a slight glare.

"I was so shaken up from the day I went on a walk that night, and that's when I saw Aeton and Maiara. You told her to be brave for you. I remember you calling her Mai." I explain.

"That's right…" Aeton says back, somewhat surprised.

"And then you were outside my father's shop later weren't you? On your way back from getting her on the truck, you came by my house." I continue to put things together.

"How do you know that was me?" Aeton asks.

"The way you were standing. I knew it was familiar when I saw you standing there tonight." I reply, my whole family looking back and forth between Aeton and me.

"Why did she have to go? Maiara, I mean, if you don't exist then she wouldn't either would she?" Clem chimes in, finally shaking off the shock of the conversation.

"I can't explain why, but she felt like she had to go." Aeton says back with pain in his voice.

"She wanted to go?" My mother inquires.

"It was more like she had to…I, I can't explain it." Aeton chokes.

"So she doesn't exist really either then?" Reg says slowly.

"Phoibe? No, she doesn't, that's why nobody has noticed her absence at work."

"Don't they notice your names?" Reg asks.

"No. There are others in Nirvana who have the same names."

"And your last name?" Clem says.

"I don't use it. Not many things require it."

"What about Phoibe's family then?" Reg asks. "What became of them?"

"Her family is fine. The officers never identified her that day. Besides, they had no reason to take out her family for what happened with my father. I imagine she contacted them somehow after she left us at Sibylla's."

I am stunned that Aeton knows Sibylla, she never mentioned being acquainted with him once in all the times we talked, adding to the mystery of her. I am thinking this over when another thought comes to me.

"Aeton, you just signed yourself into the war, you wouldn't have to be in it had you not come here tonight!"

"I promised to see you tonight Aella, besides if I don't fight that makes me a coward."

"It doesn't make you a coward! I won't let you put yourself at risk like that!" I am so confused at how calm Aeton is being about the whole situation.

"Well, unfortunately, you don't have a whole lot of say in the matter. I'm going to fight. I've already made my decision, besides I told you that we'd be in the same regiment. What do the assignment papers say Mr. Jadim?"

My father, who has been just listening to the conversation up to this point, begins to examine the small stack of papers that had been given to him by the officers. He hands them out to us according to the name that has been scrawled on the top of each one.

"I am in Regiment B." I say immediately turning my attention to Aeton who quickly develops a smile and nods his head to let me know we will be together.

Aeton had been so sure of it to the point where is seemed as though he already knew. The thought of how he could have guessed is quickly pushed out of my head by the overwhelming joy of at least getting to be together.

"I'm in E." Reg says softly.

"Me too son." My father says lifting his eyes to meet my mother's in a promise to protect Reg.

"Looks like I'll be stuck with you two." Clem interjects as he gestures to my father and Reg in an attempt to lighten the mood a bit.

"Elias, how about you take Reg and Clem into the kitchen and read your instructions to them. You should have enough candles, but if you need more you know where to find them. I will read to Aella and Aeton." My mother tells my father in an anxious voice.

"Alright Candra." He answers as he rises and heads for the door, but stops before he leaves. "We are going to be alright." He says.

"You know that don't you? I will take care of the boys, and no doubt Aeton will look after Aella. This rebel army can't be too big, perhaps we won't even see battle."

My mother nods, and then approaches Aeton and me to start reading. I hand over my paper, and she begins.

"You have been assigned to Regiment B. Tomorrow morning you will be required to meet on the northern outskirts of town just before the forest line. We will move out by sunup so you will need to be there well before to check in. Bring nothing with you, you will be provided a uniform and also be issued a pack full of any supplies you will need on the journey when you check in. Failure to be on time will result in serious punishment. Woden is working together to save our world." My mother stops, and takes a close look at the two of us. "Get some sleep, you will be up early tomorrow, and this may be the last night of good solid sleep you get for a while. Aeton you can take Phoibe's cot. Goodnight."

I can tell that she left with such briskness to avoid having us see her cry. My heart aches at the sight of her distraught face, and I wish to hug her, but I simply do as she says. As I begin to climb under my covers, Aeton takes a seat on the side of my cot.

"Do you trust me?" He asks intently.

"Of course I trust you Aeton." I answer, placing my hand on his face, which he takes hold of, and presses it firmly to his cheek.

"Good." He says as he leans in and kisses me.

Never in my life have I felt the way I do when his lips meet mine. After a moment, he pulls back, looks me straight in the eyes and takes both my hands in his.

"I promise that I won't let anything happen to you. I will protect you with my life. Aella, I care a whole lot for you, and I am not about to let you get hurt. I swear that I will get you back home to your family one day."

When he says this I throw my arms around his neck and wish that I would never have to let go.

"Thank you." I whisper as I hug him tightly.

"I'll do whatever it takes to keep you safe, just try to stay out of trouble for me would you?" I can't help but laugh a little through my tears.

"I'm not making any promises." I answer jokingly.

Eventually he releases his grip on my and kisses me on the cheek before making his way over to Phoibe's cot.

"Where are you meting tomorrow?" Clem asks instantly, as he and Reg renter the room.

"Northern outskirts, you?" Aeton answers.

"The square. Father thinks they are sending us in waves."

I drift off listening to the sound of their voices as they continue to discuss the war, hoping silently that Aeton will be as right about everything being okay as he was about us ending up in the same regiment.

9

The weight of what we were about to do hits me as Aeton and I walk hand in hand up to where the rest of those who have been assigned to Regiment B are sitting around. I choke back the few tears I have left after a morning filled with heartbreaking goodbyes to each member of my family.

The sky is still gray, as the sun has yet to make an appearance, and a soft chill lies on my skin as I let go of Aeton's hand to wrap my arms tightly around myself. I take a look around at some of the other people in our regiment and recognize a few here and there. But something about the people sticks out to me, particularly the men. One man I see has a severe limp that makes his walking rather unsteady and keeps him from moving very fast. Another man I see is missing an arm, and another has someone leading him along as though he is hardly able to see.

"Aeton, how will those men be of any use in war? Damon said that would take only the older men that they saw fit, and there is no way those men are fit for war." I say to Aeton.

"I'm sure Damon doesn't really care." Aeton responds. "Honestly Aella, can you really give him credit for his word after everything that has happened?"

"No…I just, I just don't see how anyone could send someone like that into a battle that they have no way of surviving." I reply.

"After what he did to the people in the square, I don't quite see how you could expect anything other than that sort of cruelty." Aeton shakes his head at the ground.

"Name?" Asks the gruff man who is checking people in as we stop talking to each other and approach him.

"Aella Jadim."

"Name?" The man mutters again in a monotone voice.

"Aeton Jadim."

The man simply nods at us, finding our names quickly on his list, and we make our way over to where the uniforms are being handed out. We then head separately to the men and women's changing rooms that are no more than two old warehouses, to change into our uniforms. The uniforms consist of black jumpsuit made from some material I have never seen before. It has long sleeves and legs that are much too long for me so I spend some time rolling up each sleeve and leg. The jumpsuit zips up the front, and I decide to keep my own clothes on underneath although some of the women choose to leave them behind.

Printed on each jumpsuit in the upper right side is a symbol that at first appears to be our national emblem, but a closer look reveals some fairly substantial differences. Instead of the normal shield, an eye has replaced the symbol in the middle. The banner on the bottom of the shield no longer says "Working together for the betterment of Nirvana", but "Working together for the betterment of Woden". This change to the national symbol adds even more to the growing division between the regions.

I finish getting ready by replacing my worn tennis shoes on my feet, and pulling up my long hair into a low ponytail, then make my way back out of the building where Aeton is waiting. His jumpsuit seems to fit him perfectly, and it makes me wonder how ridiculous I look.

"Took you long enough. You are such a girl." He is trying to lighten the mood, but I can tell he's anxious about something.

"Well you know I was just trying to make myself look good enough for you." I say back sarcastically.

"That's kind of weird sis'." He says with a smile and a playfully punch to my arm.

"We don't really have to keep up the brother sister act, do we? I mean everyone but the officers is going to know the truth, and besides, I honestly don't think they would care either way."

"No, we don't. I just needed the name to get into the war, not to stay in it." Aeton laughs. "That outfit looks nice on you."

"Gee, thank you." I roll my eyes.

"Gosh, you don't have to seem so grateful for compliments. Keep that up and I'll just never say anything nice to you ever again. How'd you like that, hmmm?"

"I'd like that just fine." I smile sarcastically. "If fact I'd be alright if you just stopped talking to me altogether."

"You don't mean that and you know it." Aeton shoves me.

I don't respond, but simply shrug and roll my eyes again making my way to the line where officers are handing out packs to everyone. Once I get mine, I go over to where the rest of our regiment is waiting. Some are going through their packs, while others use them as pillows in an attempt to soak up a few minutes of extra sleep before we are forced to head out. I sit down and start to go through mine, watching Aeton slightly as he stands in line to get his own. I can't help but smile thinking about how he tends to be able to turn around my worst moods and make me laugh. Even in a situation as awful as the one we are in he seems to have the ability to take my mind off of the dreadful things, and allow me to focus on the fact that at least I am not being forced into this completely alone. When he finally joins me, he has an enormous smile on his face and looks at me expectantly.

"What?" I ask, making a face at him.

"Nothing. Just tell me how amazing I am." He answers.

"Hmmmm." I say before starting to look through my pack. "You know I really don't see how you can really be so awake right now. It really isn't natural."

"You're just being grouchy, and here I'm simply trying to make the most of a rainy day…."

"It's not raining." I say with a straight face.

"And you are absolutely no fun at all." Aeton replies with a frustrated frown.

"And you seem to be rather confused about the weather." I smirk.

"Alright Aella, I see how it is. Oh well I guess I won't give you your surprise."

"Okay." I tell him with as much indifference in my tone as I can manage without cracking a smile this time.

"Okay, fine." He says back shrugging his shoulders, his crooked smile crossing his bright face. "Then I guess I'll just give this to someone else."

I turn to see he has pulled a necklace out of his pocket. It's a beautiful necklace. The pendant is a small white jewel that glistens in the first few rays of sunlight like a star on a summer night, hanging on a thin silver chain. My eyes widen at the sight, and I turn to meet Aeton's smiling eyes.

"Oh so you do want this huh?" He says before holding it out to me. "Eh, I guess I don't have anyone better to give it to."

"Wow, you sure as heck can ruin a moment, huh?" I laugh, turning the small pendant over in my hands.

"Me? What about you, with all your indifferent comments?"

"I'm just being difficult. It's beautiful." I say sincerely as I put it around my neck and then spend a moment admiring it, turning it over and over with my fingers.

"What, I don't get a hug or anything?" Aeton smiles as he opens up his arms for me to embrace him, and I throw my arms around his neck.

"Thank you." I whisper.

"I though I would give you something special." Aeton says, admiring the shining pendant.

"Aeton, it's gorgeous." I smile.

"I'm glad you like it, Clem said you would."

My smile doesn't fade until the harsh voice of a man who appears to be in charge breaks into my moment of joy.

"My name is Cethin, your regiment leader. Failure to follow my instructions to the letter will result in severe and immediate punishment. I will not tolerate any lazy soldiers; I will not tolerate any form of disrespect to me, any of my men or to any of your fellow soldiers. You will do exactly as I say as soon as I say it. If I give you a command, you will not question it. If you choose to attempt desertion from this army, you will be found out, tracked down and killed. Do I make myself perfectly clear?"

We all nod our heads immediately, for fear of getting on Cethin's bad side. He is one of the most intimidating men I have ever seen in my entire life. He is tall and muscular, with a face that appears to have been crafted out of iron. A scar runs down the left side of his face from just above his eyebrow to the middle of his cheek. His left eye seems as though it was damaged by whatever caused the scar as well, leaving it wandering as his other one focuses intently forward giving him an eerie appearance. His hair is black as night and slicked back out of his face. Cethin and his men all have guns, while we have only been provided an array of knives, swords, bows, and axes. Although we outnumber the Allure men at least four to one, it is obvious to all of us from the get go that we do not posses even the slightest hope of ever overpowering them.

"Collect your packs. We are moving out." Cethin says once he has given a brief moment for his words to sink in.

We all begin to rise and fall in behind Cethin and his second in command, a man who is equally as intimidating as Cethin, and resembles him enough to be his brother. We head off straight towards the Melaine Forest, and though there is apprehension among us, nobody exchanges more that a worried glance to each other. Everyone is incredibly quiet for what seems like hours, the only sound any of us dare to make is the sound of our marching feet. Even the officers that walk with us keep quiet, their eyes constantly searching the trees, as if expecting something horrific to appear. The only words come from Cethin as he calls out the occasional order to us, which we follow without the slightest hesitation, tired as we are.

"Stupid." Is all I can think whenever Cethin does open his mouth. "If there is anything out there he is letting it know exactly where to find all of us."

The day drags on, and our marching grows monotonous. The smell of sweat is strong among the regiment, and many of us begin to stumble and slow down. By nightfall everyone is more than ready to make camp, but the command to stop for the night simply doesn't come. It feels as though I have the weight of the world on my shoulders as I trudge steadily alongside the others, and the stars and the moon begin to grow brighter in the sky. As the stars grow brighter the fear of what lurks in the shadows on the forest grows stronger and stronger among us, and the rising tension is almost tangible. At least the fear keeps us more awake. The heat of the afternoon has left with the sun, and the moon brings an icy blanket with it that falls silently over the woods. The chill of the night makes breathing hard and dries out my throat, but when I reach for my water jug I find it empty, unaware that I had drunk so much of my water.

"Have some of mine." Acton offers immediately.

"No, no. I'll be fine." I say as I push back his outstretched hand, which he retracts reluctantly.

The night begins to grow blacker as the hours pass, and we continue to walk. Exhaustion and thirst seem to have a firm hold on each and every one of the members of our regiment. Even the Allure officers have begun to slow down and their excellent posture present that morning is nowhere to be found. Suddenly the sound of Cethin's voice fills the air, commanding us to halt, which we all do gratefully.

"You are going to be allowed a brief break. There is a lake just a few yards before you where you are advised to make fires and boil water to refill your jugs. You have one hour for this break. Sleep if you wish, but know, you are to be back here ready to go on time. If you fail to make it in time, you will face consequences. If you try to run, we will catch you, and as promised you will be killed without questioning. Your hour starts now."

The regiment quickly breaks its sloppy formation as people make their way down to the lake or into the surrounding forest to rest, but there is a timid air about everyone. Aeton and I choose to head for the lake, where I effortless get a fire started for us as I've done so many times in my fathers shop using a small box of matches from my pack. Aeton goes to fetch some water after I finish, and as I wait for him, I notice that others are having trouble making fires so I make my way over to them one by one. When I return, our water has begun to boil slightly.

"I have never walked so much in one day." I say as I take a seat next to Aeton.

He smiles at me, and I smile back before leaning over and placing my head in my hands. I stay there for a moment, thinking I could probably fall asleep right then, but instead I lift up for a moment before collapsing on my back. A blanket of leaves lies beneath me as I gaze up at the stars through the branches of a nearby tree.

"You alright over there?" Aeton says in his seemingly ever-calm manor.

"Mmm hmm. I just still can't believe that we're here you know. I mean we're headed to war, something that has never happened here before. War means that people are going to die, people we know, Aeton."

"You should probably try and get some sleep, I'll wake you up when it's time to go, and I will fill up your water jug too." Aeton says as he makes his way to his feet and brushes himself off.

"I don't know if I'll be able to fall asleep in this awful place." I respond, sitting up and glancing around at the surrounding trees timidly. "It's terrible enough being in here during the day."

"I'll look out for you. You need the rest." Aeton smiles.

"What about you?" I ask quietly.

"I'll be fine, now get some rest. You don't have too much longer." Aeton tries to be reassuring about his own condition, but I can hardly stand the thought of him not getting to rest.

Reluctantly I let my head fall back to the earth, and I close my eyes. Hard as the ground is, I am asleep in an instant, and I sleep hard. So hard, in fact, that when Aeton wakes me up I don't remember having any nightmares, something that I can't say happens often, but I figure it is due to the brief nature of my rest.

People are slowly trickling into the small opening in the woods where we had dispersed from earlier, each one of their faces saying the same thing; an hour was not long enough. Even the officers drag their feet as we are all forced to return to formation.

Boredom makes the walking worse. Some choose to eat the food that came in their packs as they walk, to give them something to do. Others try to grab leaves of every tree they pass, and some find rocks to kick along before them.

A shrill call of a far off creature wakes us all up for a moment, and the quiet murmurs cease for a time before picking back up again. Not ten minutes later though another call rings out through the cold air, only this time it sounds as though it is much closer. The air then grows remarkably quiet, and I feel as though everyone must be able to hear my heart as it pounds heavily in my chest.

Suddenly the trees seem to come alive above us as a flock of birds that have been residing there takes flight, filling the air with the sound of rustling leaves, flapping wings, and harsh squawking. Our entire regiment seems to be looking up when the screaming starts at the back of the regiment. The screams soon become mixed with wicked sounding howling. Even from the front of the regiment we can see the pack of wolf like creatures as they emerge from the dark and descend upon us.

"Run!" Cethin calls out, but he didn't have to tell us to do so, for the moment the screaming starts we begin to advance full speed ahead.

My heavy pack beats hard against my back, and I feel as though I cannot get my legs to move fast enough. The howling continues behind us, and I cannot keep myself from glancing behind me a moment. My eyes fix instantly on several of the huge creatures with fangs as long as my fingers sprinting up behind us. I shriek as one of them catches a man by the leg and drags him backwards as he sends out a scream that sends chills down my spine.

"Aella, don't look back, just run!" Aeton shouts at me.

The Allure officers that seemed so menacing before now seem to be on an equal level with us as we all run for our lives through the deep darkness that surrounds us. My feet fall upon the ground with thundering force as I push myself to go faster and faster to keep up with the others. Tears begin to stream down my cheeks as the bloodcurdling screams continue as our regiment is picked apart. Aeton is just a little bit ahead of me when a tree root catches his foot. He comes down with a harsh thud on the ground in front of him.

"Aeton!" I yell, coming to a screeching halt to help him up.

I reach his side and pull him to his feet with trembling hands. We instantly take off again, but now the creatures are so close behind us that it seems as though I can feel the heat of their breath on my back. A gunshot fills the air in the next moment and a warm liquid lands on the back of my neck followed by a pained whimper. Aeton and I look ahead to see one of the Allure men has stopped dead in his tracks, and his gun pointed right between us. Hearing the sound, more Allure men come to a stop and turn on the beasts in pursuit of us. Aeton makes me keep running until we are beyond the line the officers have created between the rest of the regiment and the pack of wolves. Others that had fallen behind duck between the line as well to avoid the shower of bullets they are dishing out. More and more shots, whimpers and howls crawl up into the night sky. Then suddenly all of the sounds stop, leaving nothing more than a ringing in the air. Timidly we all look around, our backs only to each other as we stare out into the night for fear of more terrors that may emerge. My heart continues to pound, and, for a time, the only sound is that of our breathing.

"We move on." Cethin calls out breathlessly after a moment. The groans of the regiment in response are not received well.

"When I give an order I expect it to be followed. Did I not make myself clear before? We have to get clear of these bodies before we can make camp. Staying here would be like serving ourselves to whatever other forsaken beasts come out of these woods."

Even though we all know that Cethin is correct, no one has any will to advance any further into the forest that has become even more like hell than it was before. The Allure officers only take a moment to exchange glances with each other before slowly starting to move backwards, their guns still pointed out into the night in order to protect the rest of us.

It seems like an eternity before we have gotten far enough away from the site of the attack to satisfy Cethin. He doesn't call out a command this time, but instead just stops so that we do not call any more attention to ourselves than we have to. Everyone falls into the small clearing that we've come to and clumps into the middle. None of us want to be the ones closest to the edge, but the Allure officers assume a position in a circle around us. They provide at least a small sense of security, but even though we are told we can sleep, hardly any of us are able to do so. Aeton holds my trembling head against his firm chest, and does his best to calm me down.

"What were those things?" I ask though a trembling voice.

"Faelens. They're like wolves obviously, but much bigger. Their jaws are incredibly powerful, and as you saw, they're far from slow for their size. If you get bitten by one, you might as well just let it kill you rather than get away because one way or another you will die."

"What do you mean?"

"Their bites are venomous, like a snake bite is." Aeton responds plainly.

"What about the other things that they talk about being in here? Like living trees and terrible plants?"

"I'm no expert, but some elements of this place seem to be much more common than others. You've heard the stories, and most of them aren't about the plants, they're about the creatures."

"I want to go home." I say quietly.

"I know, Aella. I know." He responds, stroking my hair gingerly with one hand and holding one of my hands tightly with the other. "I know."

"I'm scared Aeton."

"I know, we all are. Nobody here expects you not to be scared right now. We've been through hell, and we haven't even been gone a full day. No matter what happens though Aella, I will never leave your side. That is a promise I never intend to break."

"We could have very well died back there. If that officer hadn't turned around to kill that thing, we would have had no chance." I shutter at the thought.

"Now what good is it going to do for you to get upset over something that didn't happen? That officer did turn around, and we are both here safe now, and that's all that matters. Thank you for coming back for me. You are a brave person Ell, but would you do me a favor next time and just do your best to save yourself instead?"

"If one of us is getting out of here alive both of us are." I say.

"You're impossible." Aeton kisses my forehead. "Now how about you try to rest, hmm?"

"You're the one who hasn't slept since we left home. I'll stay up, you take a turn to rest." I say sternly. "I'm too shaken up to sleep anyway."

"How about you both try to rest, and I'll be sure to wake you up when they make us move out again. I'm used to running on little sleep, and I got a good rest in at our last stop." A man sitting next to us leans over and tells us.

"Thank you, sir." Aeton smiles with relief, and it is easy to tell that he is far more tired than he had let on to be.

"Thank you." I echo, and then Aeton and I shift to lie down, using our packs as pillows. I pull myself close to Aeton, and he puts his arm around me to pull me close.

"It's going to be okay Aella, I promise." He whispers in my ear, and I try my best to believe it as I drift off to sleep.

10

Aeton shifts causing me to spring awake. Looking around, I
see that most of the regiment is still asleep. The kind man that had
promised to wake us up if we started to move out sits looking out into
the forest with a dazed look on his face. The pink sky makes the events
of last night seem like they would be impossible. The forest that
surrounds us seems almost peaceful, and I can't help but think back to
when Aeton had said that the evil things only come out at night in the
Melaine Forest. He had joked then, but it had become our horrifying
reality.

The Allure officers have all fallen into a sitting position now,
and as I look at them, I can't hate them like I did the previous
morning. They had turned from being monsters into heroes. They had
risked their lives by facing the pack of beasts that pursued us, and if it
hadn't been for them, our losses would have been far more severe. My
mind travels to those that we lost, and I think almost instantly of the
three men that I saw the morning before, those that hardly seemed
suited for something like this and I doubt that they survived the night.

As I scan the sleeping crowd around us, I catch sight of Cethin as he rises slowly from the ground and stretches his back. He lifts his long arms over his head and examines the sight that lies before him. His good eye seems to have a look that is almost pity in it when he opens his mouth to speak.

"Time to move out." He says in a tone that is much less harsh than it has been in the past. Anyone who has heard him begins shaking his or her neighbors awake, and though we are slow to do so, finally we all make it to our feet.

Marching forward we stick close to one another. The officers walk around the perimeter of our tired group. Everyone seems to have much more respect for them now, and despite the events of the night past, there seems a considerable decrease in tension among us now.

After a while, the scenery begins to change. The trees get taller but less ominous. No longer does dark moss hang from their branches casting shadows on the ground. The morning sun feels terrific in comparison to the chill of the night, but I know it will not be pleasant for long.

"We aren't in Melaine anymore." Aeton says after a while.

"How do you know?" I ask.

"The trees, can't you tell they've changed? Only in the Melaine Forests is there a certain kind of trees, but there aren't any here. We should be much safer now." Aeton does his best to smile, and I try my best to do the same.

About midhour, we are allowed a brief rest as we were the day before, and as the shock of the last night starts to wear off, Cethin starts to harden once more. After our rest, he makes us check in so that he can total up the number of casualties caused by the attack on us. He comes up with a list of twenty people.

"Don't you think it's possible that some of them just ran off when all of the confusion started?" I ask Aeton as we start walking again.

"Would you have gone off on your own during that?" He responds.

"No, I suppose not." I think it over. "Twenty is so many, and we haven't even seen a battle yet.

* * * * *

The next ten days consist of about the same routine as the days prior. Walking for hours and hours followed by brief breaks. The only thing that changes is the breaks do become more frequent, which makes things a little easier, but with each day patience diminishes. With each stop, I wish more and more to remain on a break forever, and it grows harder to return to walking.

There is little talk among us now as we all try to save our breath for walking. The small amount of talk that does happen only occurs during breaks now, but even that is limited as people try to get as much sleep as possible. More reality of our situation sets in when several members of the regiment start to get ill and die. The bodies of the first two women to go are left under a tree for the buzzards since Cethin refused to let us bury them. At least they were lucky enough to die in their sleep, for some that grew ill shortly after were shot instantly so they wouldn't slow us down any more than we already had been.

Cethin's orders were carried out by the Allure officers, whom many of us had grown fond of after our first night, but as Cethin grows harder, so do they as they fear their leader greatly.

Ten days and death has already set in. We move east towards the shoreline, and for that reason do not come into contact with any form of true civilization. Aeton and I speak briefly with one of the soldiers on a break one day, and he explains that Cethin has been instructed to take us on a wide route to avoid coming in contact with any of the rebel Aject forces. We do not get to finish our conversation with him though because when he sees the three of us talking Cethin makes a point of finding something for the soldier to do.

My heart breaks at the cruelty with which we have been treated to bring the death upon us at such a rapid rate. I begin to fear even opening my mouth for the slightest cough, not knowing what Cethin would have done to me. Many simply begin to lose the will to live and ask what there is to live for in a situation like ours. The only thing that keeps me going is Aeton. Each day seems more terrible than the one before, and fatigue doesn't begin to cover the effects of our conditions. A large number of people already have gone trough the limited supply of food we were rationed, bringing others to share and thus leaving an even greater number of us hungry. Life seems to slip farther and farther away, and I fear that this is only the beginning.

11

It is Aeton's turn to rest at this stop, and I sit up watching the flames of our small fire as they dance. The power and grace of fire captivates me. The way it can be beautiful yet so deadly and destructive. I begin to think that its bright shades of red and orange could never be captured by any man made colors when the images of Damon and Cari's tattoos find their way into my mind. I quickly shake them out of my mind as people start to rise around me and I know it is time to wake Aeton and move out.

Our break began just before midhour, and the air was refreshing then, but the sun has risen now and I imagine it must be well into the afternoon. As thin as our jumpsuit are I still begin to grow hot and beads of sweat begin to form on my forehead. I turn to Aeton who is walking steadily along beside me and see that he has begun to get hot too. He reaches for his water jug that is hooked to the side of his backpack, and I notice that it is nearly empty. He looks tired and as though he is struggling to keep moving. Just as I turn to retrieve my water jug for him, I hear a shout from behind me. I spin around to find

Aeton on the ground holding his hand over his right eye. Orfeo stands over him with a look of hatred on his face. I am surprised to see him, as I hadn't noticed him at all in the past ten days. He snarls at me when he catches me looking at him, and without so much as a second thought I run at him and shove him backwards.

"Oh good, someone wants to be just like her big brother!" He yells coming at me, pulling out his knife.

Before he can reach me the officers around us have taken hold of our arms to restrain us, and two more are lifting Aeton to his feet. A moment later Cethin appears before us, his mouth pulled into a deep frown. One of his men hands him Orfeo's knife, which he begins to turn over in his hands.

"So, which one of you would like to tell me why we have had to stop moving forward? Which one of you would like to be responsible for this delay?" His eye travels from Aeton's, to mine and then on to Orfeo's.

"This," He says holding up the knife in his hands. "Belongs to you. Is that correct?"

Orfeo tilts his head to the side, and a defiant look comes into his eyes. This enrages Cethin who quickly lunges forward, placing the knife against Orfeo's neck. Instantly Orfeo's look of defiance turns to one of fear.

"Yes." He chokes out as Cethin begins to press harder. "Yes!!" He screams.

"Right, now would you like to tell me what you planned to do to this girl?" Cethin says gesturing to me with his free hand, not releasing any pressure on the knife.

"Her friend there was walking slow and kept tripping me up, so I though it best to punish him for being disrespectful and lazy. I know him from working in the forest; he has a history of disrespect. Then that girl comes at me acting all crazy and tries to kill me with her own knife, but she put it away before your men reached us. She's trouble as well, her whole family is. Her big brute of a brother came near to killing me on several occasions. She is no different from him, no different at all."

"Ah." Cethin begins to move towards me. "Now young lady, would you tell me what happened?"

"My friend was running out of water, so I reached for my own jug to give him. When I turned around, Orfeo had knocked him to the ground and was standing over him so I shoved him away, sir." I answer, disgusted by how easily Orfeo was able to lie.

Cethin listens to me, scrutinizing my every word, but when I finish talking his eyes start to smile.

"Get him out of here." He says motioning to Orfeo, and a feeling of relief floods my body. Orfeo yells profanities as he is pulled away, but his shouts soon cease following the sound of a gunshot.

"Don't get too happy sweetheart, your friend here is still going to pay for his laziness." My heart races as I imagine what Cethin means by pay. "Oh don't worry, I won't kill him. He means quite a bit to you, huh?" He doesn't wait for a response. "Of course, he means something to you. I've been watching you. Well honey, he is going to come with us now, you can have him back in the morning."

I turn to Aeton with fear in my eyes as they begin to drag him away, but Cethin pulls me around to face him. As soon as I am turned towards him, he rears back and slaps my face.

"Now you listen, and you listen good." He takes my stinging face in one of his large, rough hands and squeezes it tightly. "If you dare get involved in any more fights I will kill you, understand? I was merciful to you this time but don't you dare think that's going to continue. Orfeo was already on his second strike after being late the morning we left your miserable excuse for a home, and now you and your friend are on yours. If I hear so much as a peep out of that pretty, little mouth of yours before we reach camp tonight, you will regret it." He twists my face to the side before pushing me away from him and walking away.

As soon as he is gone I put my hand on my face, it is hot, and I'm certain it will bruise. I spend the rest of the day walking alone and in silence. Just before nightfall we get the order to stop, and for the first time, we are told to set up a semi permanent camp. The news of potential for a full nights sleep brings smiles and life to the tired faces of the majority of the regiment, but my face remains full of worry. As I set up a tent with several other women I look around for Aeton, but have no luck finding him. Each of our packs has a sleeping bag on it, and the other women and I take turns going into the tent and setting ours out where we wish to sleep. I let everyone else go first so that I don't miss Aeton. After almost an hour of sitting and waiting, I reluctantly enter the tent and set up my sleeping bag. The only space that is left is small, and in a corner, but I doubt I'll be sleeping much tonight anyway.

There is one other girl close to my age that is also in the tent, as I make up my area. She has fiery red hair that she has pulled into a high ponytail, but it still hangs all the way down to her lower back. She is thin but strong for someone her size, I remember seeing her lifting things off of a truck back before we left Woden that I wouldn't imagine she could lift. She watches me intently with her intense green eyes.

"Not much room." She says pointing at my sad attempt to straighten out my sleeping bag.

"It's alright." I look at her with a shrug.

"You're the girl who got into a bit of a fight earlier, aren't you?

"Yeah." I answer a little embarrassed. "It was hardly a fight though."

"Seen worse, huh?" She asks with a slight laugh.

"No, I just kind of wish I would have gotten to take a few more shots at him before the officers intervened." I look up at her.

"Not a fan of that man I take it?"

"Not particularly, no."

"I think you did the right thing. He deserved it. If it were me, I wouldn't have been brave enough do anything. You really must care about that boy a great deal. What is he, your brother?"

"Aeton? Oh, no he's not my brother. He signed up for the war so that he could come help protect me, because as you can see, I find it hard to stay out of trouble." I can't help but laugh a little when I think about my promise I made to Aeton before we left home to stay away from this sort of thing.

"He didn't have to sign up?" The girl asks, puzzled.

"No, um…It is quite a story honestly." I take hold of my necklace and close my eyes.

"Well, whatever the reason, he must really care for you. Did he give you that?" She asks, pointing at my necklace.

"Yeah, just the other morning actually."

"It's beautiful!" She says admiringly as she stares wide-eyed at it. "Oh wow and that ring! Did he give you that too?"

I look down at my ring that my father had given to me, and his words come into my head immediately.

"My father gave me this. He made it himself, he's a blacksmith." As I mention my father, recognition flashes on the girl's face.

"You're Aella Jadim!"

"You know me?" I ask, shocked considering the lack of time I've spent with people even remotely close to my age up until recently, and I'm sure I've never seen her before.

"You worked with my little sister at the factory, Liridona, she talks about you all the time. I'm Kenina."

The thought of Liridona makes me miss home even more, but as soon as Kenina says her sister's name I begin to recognize similarities with them.

"What regiment did she get assigned to?" I ask anxiously.

"E. All of our family is split up." There is pain in her voice as she speaks.

"My father and two brothers are in E! They know Liridona, I've spoken of her often and she's come to our home for supper, I'm sure they'll look after her!"

I can feel the relief as Kenina raises her hands into the air with joy. Just then, we hear the sound of some sort of bell coming from outside. We rise and head out of the tent, Kenina goes first and stops short as soon as she is out the door.

"What's wrong?" I ask, but just as I ask I make my way out of the tent and that's when I see it too.

12

He is tied to an upright wooden board in the middle of the campsite. I can smell his blood as the wind blows. His head hangs down so that his chin is resting on his chest. His jumpsuit has been removed, and he wears his own clothes, but they are now torn and bloody. Orfeo's body is also on display for all to see.

I gasp at the sight and begin to loose my balance as Aeton continues to let out anguish filled moans. Kenina catches me and continues to hold me up as Cethin makes his way over to the board.

"Let this be a warning to the rest of you. I did not lay out rules to have them broken or ignored; I laid them out with the expectation that they would be followed. Now I don't imagine that any of you wish to end up dead like this man here." He points to Orfeo. "Or even like my friend Aeton." Cethin slaps his hand down on Aeton's shoulder causing him to let out a horrible cry of pain, and I being to lunge forward, but Kenina catches me.

"Trust me when I say that my patience and mercy lessen as time goes on." Cethin finishes. "Now then, who wants to eat?"

His speech makes me feel sick, as if the sight of Aeton hadn't already taken my appetite away. As much as it pains me to see Aeton like this, I can't seem to take my eyes off of him. I sit down near our tent, and after she retrieves her food, Kenina rejoins me.

"You're not missing out on much." She says gesturing to the small plate of food before her. "I'm not even totally sure what this is."

I try to listen to her as she talks, but I can't seem to focus, forcing her to repeat just about every other sentence, but she doesn't seem to mind.

"I can't even imagine how you must feel right now. I've never loved anyone that way." Her eyes have fallen on Aeton, and she looks as though she might get sick at any moment.

What she says stuns me. No one has ever used the word love to describe the relationship between Aeton and me before, and it makes me begin to think. I sit in silence staring at his face that is being illuminated by the firelight.

"I'm sure he'll be perfectly fine." Kenina says in a comforting way as she places her hand gently on my shoulder.

I look to the ground for a moment, fighting tears, then soon move my eyes back to Aeton.

"Well staring at him isn't going to help make you feel any better. Aella, come on let's go inside. It's late anyway." She begins to make her way to her feet as she speaks and starts to pull me up with her.

"You go ahead, I'll be there in a minute." I say back trying to make myself as heavy as possible as she yanks me upward.

"No, look this isn't good for you. What is staring at him going to do anyhow?"

"You're right." I shake my head and force myself to get to my feet, and as I do my stomach begins to growl and I wish silently that I had eaten.

"Grabbed this for you." Kenina says with a small smile as she throws me a large piece of bread.

"Do you know how much trouble you could get in for…" I start but before I can finish she cuts in.

"I know, but it's not a big deal. Honestly, I'll be fine."

I can't help the giant smile that appears on my face. I have only known Kenina for a mater of hours, and I already feel as though we've been close friends for a while. We make our way into the tent to find that none of the other women have made it back from dinner yet. We swiftly rearrange my sleeping bag so that it is next to Kenina's. We lie there talking for a while and begin to drift off just as the other women begin to appear. It isn't long before Kenina is asleep, and I'm surprised when my own eyes seal tightly as I too fall asleep.

* * * * *

The tent is dark as I take a look around to make sure that no one else is awake, and fortunately all the women are sleeping soundly. I shake my head as I begin to replay my dream, for the first time in as long as I can remember it is different. I am running from something, like normal, but this time Aeton and Kenina are at my sides. We make our way through the densely packed trees and thick underbrush, but darkness is not what peruses us. The forest is different this time as well, and it seems as though it will never end. We run for what seems like ages. Then suddenly, a large, extravagant palace comes into view. I recognize it as Scheol from pictures I have seen in school, and that's where the dream ends. The dream leaves me with so many questions I can hardly bring myself to focus on one. As my hand finds the small pendant around my neck my mind stops swimming in its sea of questions, and I begin to make my way quietly to the door of the tent. I dodge the other women the best I can, taking small, careful steps as I move gradually along. After several close calls due to missteps, I make it to the door and begin unzipping it with care.

When the door is just open enough for me to stick my head out I take a deep and relived breath as I see the complete lack of officers in the camp. Although I still can't believe or explain my actions, I continue unzipping the tent. I just get it open enough to slip out when I hear a small noise from behind me in the tent.

"Aella?" Kenina's voice calls quietly out to me.

I turn to find her standing just behind me, and, upon finding her there, I jump slightly, coming close to losing my balance.

"Where are you going?"

"I can't explain it. I had a dream…I have to go now."

I turn and make my way out the door, taking a few quiet steps forward to look for any officers that I couldn't see from the tent door, but find none. Turning around, I find Kenina zipping up the last bit of the tent door.

"So, what's the plan?" Her face is full of determination, and I know that nothing I say will persuade her to let me continue on without including her.

Without answering, I begin to make my way towards the post that Aeton is still tied too, and gesture for her to follow.

"Aeton?" I say as we reach him. I wait a while before repeating his name, this time a little louder than the first.

"Aeton?" I begin to panic when he doesn't answer and turn to Kenina for help.

"What are you looking at me for?" She asks. "I don't know what to do."

I look back at Aeton and then before I even realize what I am doing, I yank the pendant from around my neck and thrust it into his hand, using my own hand to wrap his cold fingers tightly around it. Almost instantly the color begins to return to Aeton's body, and my hand that is still wrapped around his begins to feel the warmth of life. He slowly lifts his head and gasps for air, and after another moment he begins to open his eyes. I can hardly contain my excitement as I throw my arms around him after untying the ropes confining him.

"You figured it out." Aeton says to me as I loosen my grip.

"Figured what out?" Kenina asks, looking back and forth between the two of us.

"The dream I sent to her and the power of the necklace."

"Power of the huh?" Kenina shakes her head.

At the mention of the necklace I look at Aeton expectantly, and his face fills with question. My glance moves to his hand that had been holding the necklace, but he now holds nothing.

"Where did it go?" I ask sadly and genuinely confused.

"What happened to your eye?" He returns my question with one of his own and reaches up and softly touches my face.

"That's not important. What's going on?" I say sternly.

Before he can answer the question, a noise from a short distance away brings the three of us back to the reality of our situation.

"I'll explain on the way." Aeton says, now seeming to be back to his old self, and I notice all of his cuts and bruises are virtually gone.

"The way where?" Kenina asks, holding back.

Aeton stays silent as he grabs Kenina and me both by our arms and begins to pull us hastily towards the tree line. Just as we make it to cover, I turn to see six officers make their way back into the center of the camp. Upon finding Aeton missing they begin to sound the alarm and all at once the camp roars to life. It grows farther in the distance and becomes almost invisible between the trees. My heart races as we leave our regiment behind and run full force ahead through the trees. I glance back and forth at Aeton and Kenina's determined faces, and I realize that my dream has suddenly turned into my reality.

13

There are so many things that don't add up, and as I run that is all I can think about. I keep on expecting Scheol to come into view as it did in my dream, but it never does. Instead, the forest continues to surround us. My breath is growing short, but I dare not stop running for fear of the officers that may be following us.

"Aella…" Aeton says as he suddenly comes to a stop.

"What is going on?" I stop and look at him, my voice coming out in an extremely serious and harsh tone I've never used with him before.

"I know you're a little confused right now Ell, I just need you to trust me. Please, look I know I haven't been completely honest with you and I know you are scared, but I really need you to save your questions. I promise I will explain as soon as I can."

"A little confused, Aeton?" I take a step back.

"Guys, is this really the best time to discuss..." Kenina asks.

"She's right. You'll understand soon." Aeton finishes.

We take off once again through the woods, moving as quickly as possible with Aeton in the lead. The sun is slowly beginning to make its way into the sky, casting shadows on the ground and sending a variety of colors into the slowly lightening sky. It's only when I see the sun that I realize which direction we are traveling in. In my dream, we were heading north in the direction of Scheol, and I can't figure out why Aeton is leading us east.

Suddenly up ahead I see what appears to be a break in the dense trees. We come into a small meadow. Everywhere I look I see debris from what appears to have been a large stone building. Aeton seems to be searching for something amongst the rubble, he keeps mumbling to himself as he picks around. Kenina and I take advantage of the break, not knowing how long it will last, leaning against large stones and attempting to catch our breath.

"Over here." Aeton calls after a few minutes, and motions for us to join him.

We walk quickly over to where he stands, dodging stones as we walk. When we reach him, he points to a small door that is lying on the ground.

"This is it."

"This? What is this?" Kenina asks as if she's read my mind.

"I thought we had a deal about asking questions." Aeton says as he bends down and after a short struggle, opens the door. I am astonished when it opens to reveal a staircase. I can only see the top couple of stairs, as the rest of them are concealed by darkness.

Looking to Aeton, I realize that he plans for us to go down the stairs, but not knowing what lies at the bottom of the stairs, I hesitate. Without so much as a word, Aeton turns and with a flick of the wrist, he somehow causes the whole staircase to become illuminated by a series of torches along the walls. Before I can even process what has happened, Aeton is making his way down the moss-encrusted steps. Kenina is the next to begin to make her way down, followed after a moment by me. The staircase is longer than I had anticipated and I feel the air growing colder as we gradually descend. I stumble a time or two as I walk down the decrepit staircase as pieces of it have chipped away, and moss has come in to cover up the faulty points.

When we reach the bottom of the staircase we find ourselves face to face with more blackness, but it doesn't stay long. Aeton brings to life the torches that are spread about the now visible room. It's much larger than one would guess, and I'm surprised to see a small amount of furniture. Once he makes sure we are settled in, Aeton walks over to the staircase and I hear the door slam shut above us, and the room grows dimmer as the torches leading down into the cellar go out.

"We'll stay here until nightfall, and then we will head out towards Aject. It will be safe here, trust me nobody will find us." Aeton tells us with only partial confidence in his voice. I look at him and then at Kenina, who turns her eyes towards Aeton as she joins me on the small, dust-covered sofa.

"I guess you'll be wanting an explanation right about now?" Aeton says with a slight smile. "Alright, so what do you want to know?"

My mind begins to sort through hundreds of questions that have been building up inside me, but before I can find one that I want answered first I blurt out;

"Everything."

"I can't tell you everything Aella." Aeton laughs. "There's far too much. But, I suppose the best way for me to begin is with an apology. Obviously the life that I have pretended to lead is not exactly the whole truth. My sister and I really did come from Aject with Phoibe, but under different circumstances than I described. There was a fire, but it had nothing to do with my parents. I never knew my mother, and as for my father, well it was somewhat impossible for him to be part of my life. That's a totally different story."

I look at him with pain in my eyes, and he returns my look with an apologetic one of his own.

"Also, as you can tell I'm not exactly like everyone else. I have abilities that are not common." Aeton continues.

"Oh really? I thought everyone had the ability shoot fire out of their palms." Kenina looks at him with a frown.

"Well you're wrong." Aeton says back to her, trying to lighten the mood. "I am a member of the Basir, we work for King Fino as his eyes and ears of what goes on in the kingdom. We can contact the king from anywhere, just as he can reach us. He commissioned us to help him keep the peace in Nirvana, and allow him to see every part of the kingdom at once. He has put in to each of us a small amount of power. It's a type of power that they once called thaumaturgy many years ago, or magic. We also serve as guardians for certain citizens, whether they have been chosen to be part of the Basir in the future or are for something far greater. "

"King Fino? You mean the man who called us into war? The man who commanded that all those children be taken away from Woden?" I ask in a sudden rage.

"Fino had nothing to do with that, honestly. He doesn't have a choice. The Enlighteners and Allure have more power than they were ever supposed to, they've become corrupt, but they're no fools. They often make themselves seem as though they are no more than the messengers. They make people hate the king based on fallacy." Aeton says back defensively. " Anyway, the Enlighteners don't know we exist. Well, they do, but they aren't as in tune with everyone who is involved or what it is we do. We know all about them, every member of the Enlighteners, as well as every member of the Allure. We know the positions they hold, and who among them are particularly powerful, and we know their mark. They don't exactly go to great lengths to conceal it. We thought we'd done a good job of keeping them from knowing about us as we know about them. The morning we were handed our uniforms I noticed the symbol on them contained our mark, an eye. Each Basir member has the same mark, it's our own, secret, sacred symbol."

As he mentions the mark, Aeton pulls back the side of his torn shirt to reveal a tattoo of an eye on his right shoulder. It is about two inches wide, and the most incredible blue I have ever seen. I look down at the symbol on my jumpsuit to compare the two, and there is no denying that they are exact matches.

"We have methods of concealing our marks, and even if one of us slipped up and they saw it, there are plenty of tattoos out there. I knew when I saw the new symbol that the Enlighteners know a great deal more about us than we had previously thought." Aeton continues to explain.

"Why would they put the symbol for a group that is against them on our uniforms?" I ask.

"I've done some thinking, and my best guess is that it's a warning to us, to let us know that they know more than we've given them credit for."

"So when did you become one of them?" Kenina interjects.

"Well, I learned about them from Phoibe. When I escaped from the fire that took our house, we didn't go directly to Woden." Aeton looks at me, but I cast my eyes towards the ground, another half-truth from before. "Phoibe took Maiara and me to Scheol and introduced us secretly to the king who made the two of us part of the Basir, and appointed Phoibe, who already was part, to show us the ropes. King Fino was stronger then, but he grows weaker with each passing day, the Enlighteners are draining his power slowly but surely."

"What do they have against the poor old man anyway?" Kenina cuts in for another question.

"They were once his advocates, but many years ago, there was a rebellion during which the Enlighteners took advantage of the power they'd been given. One of them thought he deserved to be king, he thought that King Fino wasn't using his power to it's full potential. The rebels banded together and imprisoned Fino in the palace. They have been stealing his power ever since. They joined up with the Allure, which was made up of the king's most powerful advisors, and decided to take control of the kingdom. Roles have switched a little now though. Even on those who were once their allies have turned somewhat. The Enlighteners had far more in the way of numbers than the Allure and for that reason thought they were above them. The Allure fell to basically no more than pawns."

"Cethin, was he an Enlightener?" I say, looking up again.

"Yes, but he seemed as though he was on the bottom of their food chain. Most of the newer ones are more violent. They often feel as though they have to build up a reputation for themselves, and in a sense, they're right. But no matter how horrible they are, they will never reach a position that is higher than the one Damon holds." Aeton answers.

"What happened during the rebellion? I mean what really went wrong?" Kenina takes her turn for another question.

"There is a great deal of back story to the why, but when it happened basically, the queen was murdered because she was powerless, they spared the princess though, Avina. They keep her confined to the palace as well, but not under near as tight a watch as the king. As far as Damon is concerned she is only alive because she sort of gives the king something to live for. And, the only reason they keep the king alive is because if he dies, so dies the power."

"I thought that magic all vanished after Nirvana was originally started. The man who saved the people, we've always been taught he was the last of his kind." I frown, now even more confused.

"That man was named Freyer, and he had a son. As long as his son lived, so would the magic. As his son grew up, he found that he wasn't always able to deal with all the power he had. With the amount of magic in his veins, he was the most powerful of the survivors, even as a child. His mother did a good job of helping him keep his abilities a secret, that's why it was believed to have been lost in the first place. He grew up, learned how to deal with power without letting it control him. He was charismatic and won over the people, and when he was only thirty years old they appointed him their king."

"King Fino." Kenina says.

"Exactly. As his kingdom grew, so did his power. He found out one day a method of transferring it to another person. He did so by accident with his mother when she grew sick. It took pressure off of him to share his power. That's when he began to share with his advisors, and thus, the Enlighteners were created. Now, they keep him just barely alive, strong enough to live, but weak enough so that he is virtually helpless. From what we've learned, their plan is to drain him as low as possible of power. Then, all the power the various Enlighteners posses will be given to Damon one day so that he can kill the king, yet be strong enough to prevent the power from being lost."

"If King Fino is the son of the man who started Nirvana, wouldn't he and the Enlighteners be dead by now?" Kenina cuts in.

"Fino's power makes him immortal. The Enlighteners though, they have other ways of staying young. They steal the lives of others to add to their own. They eat wild animals mostly, and absorb their years, but the lives of animals don't work as well as those of humans. The children they took from Woden were being removed not to see the king, but so the Enlighteners could use their lives. Being so young, those children had many years left."

"How?" Is all I can manage to say, as my heart has leapt into my throat.

"They have the ability to shift forms. They turn themselves into snakes, giant snakes, big enough to consume a good sized bear."

I had imagined what would have become of poor Koen, but my wildest thoughts did not even come close to the reality. I feel anger that anyone could be so selfish as to take the life of an innocent child in such a way. I feel pain for the horrific loss and gruesome fate that fell upon so many helpless lives. I feel hatred on those who caused this fate and a yearning for revenge boils inside of me.

"They have fangs that are almost a foot long, they're filled with a poisonous form of power that, if left in the bloodstream will begin to change the victim. But it's incredibly rare that a meal is left unfinished. You've seen one though Aella, a victim. The bear in the woods that day, it was some kind of mutation caused by the poison. Something must have stopped one of them short in the attack of that bear, and it lived." Aeton goes on. "That was the day we found Phoibe's ring, which brings me to something else, the necklace that I gave you. That gift was as genuine as it could have been, but giving you something nice wasn't my only motive. When I found out that we were going to war, I knew I was in a bit of a situation. Certain members of the Enlighteners and even the Allure can sense power in others. I didn't know if there were any such members in our regiment, so that's when I formed the necklace I gave you. It was made out of my power, contained into a small jewel, small enough so that it would go undetected by an Allure. I had you wear it to help keep my powers a secret. I was weak for a while since I drained myself so quickly. I began to have a harder time when we walked. That's why I stumbled to the point of causing the problem with Orfeo."

My heart hurts as I think of the many breaks we took when Aeton would let me sleep, and stay up to watch instead of resting himself. Only now can I see that it was even harder for him to do that than I had previously thought.

"Having kept a very small amount of my power, I was able to send you the dream, but I could only hope you would understand." Aeton smiles a little and looks up at me. "You did, and you saved us. So, now we're here, safe."

"What is this place?" I ask as I begin to think through all the information Aeton has just shared.

"I'm not quite sure actually, the king sent me a vision of it and led me here." He answers taking a look around the room.

"What exactly happened to the necklace when I gave it to you?" I ask as I get up to walk around a bit.

"I absorbed the power back into my body, and used it to heal my wounds." I nod and take the information in. Then another question pops into my mind.

"Phoibe." I say. "Do you know if she's alive?"

"No. I sure hope so, but...Why don't you try and lie down for a while? I know we have all day to sleep, but you'll need all the rest you can get. Tonight is going to be long."

I make my way to the small bed that sits in the corner of the room. A twinge of pain shoots through my heart, but the luxury of being in an actual bed soon takes over, and it isn't long before I fall fast asleep.

14

I am sitting in a field watching Koen as he runs and plays. He laughs and smiles at me, ducking down in the tall grass and coming back up a few feet away from where we went down. He begins to run towards me when several figures emerge from the surrounding forest on the opposite side of the field. Among them are Damon and Cari. They all walk slowly, and each of them wears fancy clothing, all of which is bright purple. Suddenly Cari and a man I don't recognize are upon me with speed that one could only imagine possible. They restrain me as I struggle and yell. Cari takes hold fast of my hair, forcing my face upward so my eyes fall directly on a helpless, squirming Koen who is also being restrained by another unfamiliar man.

Damon stands calmly between the two of us with an awful, devilish grin on his face. He walks towards me, his eyes scrutinizing my being as he draws nearer. His look seems to cut through me, and I feel as though he is consuming me from the inside out. Then without warning he turns and begins to move quickly towards Koen. Halfway there, he leaps into the air and when he lands he is no longer a man.

His body has transformed, and he now wears the skin of a giant snake. His black scales glisten in the sunlight revealing a purple tint as he slithers ominously forward in Koen's direction.

When he reaches his destination, he turns his head towards me, his open mouth revealing his fangs. Before I am able to process what is happening, he sinks them deep within Koen's side. Eyes filled with agonizing pain, Koen's body begins to convulse as the venom easily penetrates his blood stream, the only thing preventing him from collapsing being the firm grasp of the man behind him. Damon lets go and moves his massive head as blood starts to pour from Koen's wound and spills down his side. The sunlight shows through two large gashed holes in his thin body revealing just how much power was behind Damon's jaws. Koen's mouth opens wide as if to scream, but no noise comes out. His soundless screams continue until his body falls limp as the poison takes him, and the man who has been holding him up lets him fall to the ground.

I let out a series of helpless shrieks as I am forced to watch as Damon consumes my brother's body. When he is done, his scale-covered face turns and his terrible eyes focus on mine. My cries for help grow louder and louder as he slithers over towards where I'm being held. He gets within striking distance, and his fangs are but inches from my face, the sound of my own screams wake me up. I spring from the bed, taking a few steps forward and finding myself wrapped in Aeton's strong arms. I shake violently as my nightmare begins to play over in my head.

"It alright Aella. It was just a dream…It was just a dream." Aeton says soothingly, but his voice has almost as little power to calm me down as do his arms around me. He places his hand gingerly on the back of my head and begins to stroke my hair softly. I bury my face in his chest and try as hard as I can to shake the horribly vivid nightmare from my mind.

My feelings for Damon had turned to hate. Seeing him in my dream and being so helpless had only hardened my resolve to have revenge on him.

"We need to get to Scheol, now." I say shortly as I break away from Aeton and head for the staircase, wiping tears from my eyes.

"Aella its still the middle of the day, we have to travel by night, its safer that way."

"I don't care, I need to find him." I snarl, and Aeton garbs hold of my arm as I make it to the first stair, forcing me to face him.

"Find who?" He asks calmly.

"Damon. He has to pay for what he did to Koen and the others. Let me go."

"Damon? Aella you're kidding aren't you? I've told you what he's capable of. His power surpasses mine by a long shot, and getting to him when he is in Scheol is right up there with impossible. Other Enlighteners who are incredibly powerful constantly surround him. Marching up to the palace and calling him out is not going to fix anything. Going alone now would be suicide."

"Then I'll get people to help me." I mutter through clenched teeth. "I'll get people to help me if you won't."

"No, Aella, I didn't mean that I wouldn't help you. You just can't do this right now. You aren't ready. And I seriously doubt you would be able to get many people to help you on this. Don't you see that the whole nation is missing so much? Just tonight did what I told you not prove how brainwashed the Enlighteners have almost all of Nirvana? They have taken control and made it so the man who helped to save this nation is the one being treated like the enemy and those who follow him are being persecuted. They even have people starting to believe that all of the awful things they're doing are right. You are going to be a light in this dark nation Aella, but you can't off fighting it unprepared and uneducated because it will rip you apart. Before you know it, you could be just like the Enlighteners."

"I will never be like them Aeton." I snap.

"How many people do you know who wake up with the intention of being terrible, or if they aren't already, with the intent of allowing evil things to sway them? It may look terrible from here Aella, but sometimes people get a small taste of it and suddenly they don't find it as repulsive as they once did. Then, before they know it, they've completely lost sight of the person they were and end up where they are almost beyond any sort of help." Aeton tells me in a horribly serious tone, but there is a hint of pleading in the words.

I turn my face away from him and bite my lip. Although I know he's right, I still suppress my strong yearning for revenge.

"Fine." I say indignantly. "It's hot in here, I need to get out and get some fresh air or something."

"Sorry, Ell, going out in broad daylight is too risky. You can make it a couple more hours, cant you?" Aeton looks at me kindly.

"Well how are we going to know when it's dark enough to move if we're stuck in this hole, huh?" I ask, starting to lose my temper again.

"I'll know, trust me. Before you know it, we'll be in Scheol, and you'll have time to prepare yourself for facing Damon."

"And how long is that going to take?"

"I'm not sure, that just depends on what the king says once he gets a chance to meet you. I don't know though, it could be as little time as a few weeks to as much as years, I'm not an expert on King Fino really." Aeton laughs lightly, but suddenly I am unable to restrain my brain as it swirls into a rage. "I understand your pain, you just need to be patient."

"Years? You expect me to wait here for years? You just don't understand, do you? He killed my brother Aeton I just want to get out of here. I want him to pay. I can't believe you're doing this to me! I know you have a little reputation to uphold with your precious king, but you're not being fair. I have rights Aeton, and honestly I could not care less what King Fino's stupid plan is! You couldn't possibly understand how I feel, don't even pretend to! My little brother is dead. I am never going to see him again, and you're trying to stop me from avenging him! He didn't deserve to die, but Damon does!" My voice has reached the point of yelling and Aeton stands before me, absorbing each of my words calmly.

"Maiara didn't deserve to die either, Aella, but she did. She didn't have to die damn it, but she's gone! She did it because King Fino told her that she needed to be on one of those trucks when they pulled out of Woden. So you think I don't want that monster to pay for what he's done? You think I don't want to see each and every one of them burning in hell I do, more than anything I do! But the king has a plan, okay. No. No, I don't see how it is going to work out the way he says it will. I don't see why innocent children have to suffer in order for the plan to happen. I don't see why if he already has a plan why can't we just go ahead and skip to the end and avoid all of this."

"Aeton…" I start, chocking back tears.

"We'll continue on our way to Scheol as soon as we can tonight and when we get there maybe you'll understand a little more of this plan. Perhaps you'll even understand the whole thing the way I've never been able to. I'm sorry. Can't you see that I'm terribly sorry? I'm sorry you've had losses. I'm sorry you've had to leave your family. I'm sorry that I can't help you get what you want right now. If we could leave this hole, we would. If we could go out and get some fresh air, we would. If I could have saved all those kids, believe me no power in hell would have been able to stop me, but there are some things in this life that we have no control over. We just have to work around that. We can't always see the full plan or understand why things happen, but the king knows, he knows the future, and he knows the best way to destroy Damon. As hard as it may be we have to trust him. And as far as I can see, that may be quite the chore for you. I know it is for me!" His words come at me like knives, and I can't bring words to my mind to formulate a response.

I want so badly to say I'm sorry, to tell him that I didn't mean any of what I said, but before I can he walks off to the opposite side of the room and leans his back against the wall. As he slowly sinks to the ground, I can see the tears forming in his eyes and I feel even worse.

"Aeton I…" I start, but he cuts me off by putting up his hand for me to stop.

"Don't." He says shortly.

"I'm sorry, Aeton…Please…" I try again.

"Don't, Aella. Just don't."

My heart instantly sinks at his words. My anger should not have driven me to say what I did, and I want nothing more than to make it right. My rage had caused me to forget about Maiara, and even though he never spoke of it, I can only imagine how hard it was for Aeton to lose her. At least Koen wasn't all I had left of my family as she was to him.

I know I need to give him time to calm down before I try talking to him again, but I still hesitate a moment before going back to sit on the bed. Only now do I notice that Kenina has been asleep through everything, and I wish that I could have remained asleep as to avoid the conflict that had arisen. I try my best to get a little more sleep, I take deep breaths and close my eyes, but despite my efforts, I am unable to drift off. I begin to count the minutes as they pass, staring at the cracks in the cement ceiling of the room. After a while, I begin to lose track of the time that has passed. I turn to the side restlessly when a voice breaks the silence.

"Mind if I sit?" Aeton asks as he approaches the bed.

"No, not at all." I answer as I move into a sitting position, and as he sits, I notice how red and puffy his eyes are.

"Look, I…" I start, just as Aeton says;

"Listen…"

We both stop and look at one another, and can't help but laugh a little, instantly allowing some of the tension between us to dissipate.

"Aeton, I…What I said before, I…I didn't mean it, any of it." I choke out all at once, unable to look at him.

"Don't worry about it." He says back in a steady voice. "I understand you're scared and confused, and the fact that I haven't been honest with you can't possibly be helping that, but look I need you to trust me when I say that the king has a plan on what to do about Damon. Aella, look, there is so much that I wish I knew right now to make you understand, and make it easier for you to trust me. I wish I knew more myself, because it is just as hard for me to see why everything must be done just so. I don't like the limited knowledge I have been allowed. It's frustrating to be asked to do something and not be told why. Hell, it's infuriating. But if you can, you have to try and understand that the king has a very specific plan, and the moment people like us start to take that plan into our own hands is when things start to go wrong. So Ell, I'm begging, please. Trust me."

"I trust you, and I'm willing to do whatever you need me too. Just, please, say you'll forgive me. Aeton, I know you have no reason to…What I said, there was no reason for it. You're right, I don't understand, and that frustrates me because I'm the kind of person who likes to have the whole plan. I've kept all my emotions about Koen and everything to myself for so long. That doesn't mean that taking it all out on you was right, but…" My voice shakes as I speak and I begin to twist my ring around my finger.

"Aella, look at me." He says and puts his hands under my chin, gently forcing my face upwards. "Don't worry about it, I forgive you." His crooked smile backs up his words, and I can't help but laugh a little.

"I've acted like an idiot." I say, shaking my head at myself.

"Look, I'm sorry too. I should be the one begging you for forgiveness. Nothing I said had to be said the way it was, and if I had just been honest with you from the start, you would have no reason not to trust me in the first place." Aeton says as he takes my hands in his.

"We've both been idiots haven't we?" I laugh again.

"Yes, but at least nobody was around to see it. I mean really though, how did she sleep through this whole thing?" Aeton laughs too, pointing at Kenina. "She's been out for hours!"

"Her little sister is quite the talker, maybe she's just used to sleeping with a lot of noise." I smile halfheartedly, thinking of home.

"You miss everyone don't you?" Aeton asks, putting his arms lightly over my shoulders.

"More than anything. I've never been apart from them like this. My father went away for a few days once, there was the time when Koen was in the infirmary, and Phoibe has been gone for so long, but

I've never been away from all of them at once. I've never been truly scared that I'll never see them again." I respond quietly.

"Hey, I promised you that I'd get you home one day, and that is a promise that I have every intention of keeping." Aeton smiles and pulls me close. "You'll be back with your family before you know it."

I close my eyes and lean against his shoulder, trying my hardest to trust that he is right.

15

I wake up to find myself wrapped in Aeton's arms. I try my best not to wake him as I slowly begin to rise, but his light laughter lets me know he's already up.

"Any bad dreams?" He asks as I finish sitting up and begin to stretch my arms. His words send my mind into a frenzy as I try to remember, but as hard as I think I have no recollection of a dream, or nightmare in my case.

"No. That was quite possibly the most peaceful bit of sleep I've had in quite a long time."

"I hoped it would be." Aeton's grin lets me know that there is something he's not telling me. I raise my eyebrows and frown slightly at him.

"What?" He asks as innocently as possible, and that's when I realize what he did.

"Oh, nothing. I'm guessing that it wasn't just a coincidence. I didn't know you could do that."

"No. No, that wasn't me." Aeton beams as he is extremely satisfied with himself.

"Wow. You know you're very funny." I roll my eyes.

"I know. You don't have to tell me."

"Aeton I'm serious what did you do."

"Fine. I may or may not have done some little tricks with your mind. It's nothing. I've done it before."

"Well that's not the slightest bit creepy." I smile.

"You know sometimes I don't exactly think before I open my mouth." Aeton looks at me with humor in his eyes.

"Yeah, you must not think a whole lot." I say. "So exactly how often do you play little tricks on my head then?"

"Just when I'm trying to help get a little restful sleep. Gosh, you don't have to act so grateful, I mean really, it's no big deal."

"Are you allowed to use your powers to do that?"

"I'm not allowed to tell you that." Aeton says as he wraps his arms tightly around me and pulls me close. "I don't not think before I speak that often do I?"

"Oh, no." I breathe.

"You've had your moments too." Aeton smiles.

"You're rather annoying. You know that don't you?" I say as I look up at him.

"I think I can live with that." Aeton smiles at me again and kisses my forehead.

"Well, well, well. Shouldn't we be getting ready to go? I mean it's got to be getting close to nightfall by now, unless there's something that you two would like to finish before we go?" Kenina appears beside us, her voice filled with an overwhelming sense of sarcasm.

We both laugh quietly as we rise and begin to prepare to leave, and for the first time, I realize how incredibly hungry I am. I hear my stomach begin to growl, and judging by the looks I receive from Kenina and Aeton, I'm not the only one who heard it. Before I can say anything, Aeton has conjured up a light meal on the small table that sits on the east side of the room.

"Wow, impressive. Those powers of yours are growing on me mate." Kenina says as she makes her way to the table and takes a seat; and not waiting for us, she digs in.

"Shall we?" Aeton gestures towards the table.

The table contains a small variety of foods; bread, jam, cheese, and a small amount of ham. There is only just enough for the three of us, and it doesn't take long for each of us to eat our share. As soon as we're done, Aeton cleans up any trace of us having been it the cellar by waving his hand around the room. When he does this, items in the room seem to come alive as they find their way back to the positions we found them in.

Kenina and I begin to walk up the stairs, and Aeton brings up the rear, putting moss back on the steps where our feet have pulled it away. When we reach the top of the stairwell he has to open the door for us. When it opens, I can instantly feel the slight chill in the breeze. The stars are out and looking brighter than I've ever seen them.

"This way." Aeton calls to us as he replaces a clump of vines over the door.

We begin to walk north, and as we go the chill of the night air begins to tighten its grip around us. Thinking back to the night before I can't seem to remember being cold or not, but there was so much going through my mind before it was as though my thoughts were keeping me warm. I find myself wishing I still had a million questions running through my mind, but I have no questions now, only apprehension. And apprehension, so it would seem has no power to warm.

The light of the moon is all we have to see by, Aeton walks briskly, and it is hard to keep up with him at times. Every so often I find myself having to drastically increase my pace in order not to lose sight of him. Kenina seems to have no trouble keeping up, she looks ahead and keeps her focus there, while I constantly look from my feet to Aeton, and back again.

I am relieved when Aeton finally allows us a break. My back resting against a tree, I attempt to get my breathing back under control. Years of work in the blacksmith shop have by no means gotten me in terrific shape, and although spending time in the forest during recent weeks helped to increase my stamina, I am still far behind those who spend years there.

As I continue to struggle for air, I realize how dry my mouth is. Water has been the least of my concerns over the past twenty-four hours. The last time I had anything to drink was after I ate the bread Kenina had grabbed for me back at camp. After thinking it over, I notice Aeton hadn't provided water with the meal he created, and I begin to wonder about the limitations of his power.

"You're thirsty." Aeton says as he approaches me and leans against the tree beside me.

"A little." I answer.

"I'm sorry, but my powers only allow me so much."

"Don't worry about it, we'll find some." I say and put my hand in his as I speak, moving myself closer to him.

His body is warm and being near him takes the edge off the chill of the night. He turns his face towards mine and smiles before leaning in and kissing me on the cheek. For just a moment, the world seems to stand still as Aeton and I stand there, I think to myself. If only it could last forever. But, a sharp gust of wind takes hold of me, and screams for me to come back to reality. Aeton breaks away from me, taking his warmth with him, but leaving the burning of his lips on my cheek.

"You can't just make some appear?" Kenina asks as she kicks at the dirt beneath her feet.

"I wish, but things aren't always that easy, especially when you need them to be." Aeton shrugs and begins to walk again. "Come on, there is bound to be water on the way, it could be close."

We've taken all but two steps when the unmistakable sound of twigs and leaves breaking underfoot comes from behind us. Each of us stops mid-step and whirls around. Upon hearing the sound grow closer, we all head for cover behind nearby trees. As the figure stumbles into view, I can't help myself as I spring from behind my tree and run towards him. I reach him and throw my arms tightly around him, only to retract them quickly when I feel the warm liquid on his back. Stepping back, I look down at my hands to find them sticky with blood. With a quivering voice, I look into his eyes and mutter quietly.

"Clem?"

16

I lose my balance and stumble backwards, winding up on the ground. The smell of blood causing my head to spin in a way it never has before. Relief, felt for just a moment at the sight of my brother, turned so quickly into confusion and horror. I can't seem to process what's going on, much less react in a proper way. Clem begins to fall, but doesn't make it to the ground for Kenina is there to catch him, joined soon after by Aeton who helps her return him to a standing position. Kenina then helps me get back on my feet, but as she lets me go, the ability for my body to stand on its own still seems faulty, forcing her to take hold of my arms once more.

"Clem, are you okay?" Aeton's voice is steady, but still filled with concern. Panting and hardly audibly, Clem responds.

"I ran away. I couldn't…One found me, and I ran, but…They're coming."

Fear poisons my blood, forcing Kenina to support all my weight now. She struggles to stay on her own feet as she moves me over to a nearby tree to have it share my weight.

"How far behind you are they, do you know?" His voice filled to the brim with determination to get us all out of there alive, Aeton wraps one of Clem's arms around his shoulder, and motions for Kenina to take the other.

"A few minutes at the most." Clem chokes out.

As Kenina and Aeton drag Clem along I am able to see how dangerously slow we are going, and the need to survive begins to take over my body. I feel so utterly helpless watching them, and Kenina seems to be struggling, strong as she is. After a moment, I can hardly stand it anymore. I know I am stronger than Kenina, and in a swift motion I am able to switch places with her and take over carrying Clem. We are able to move at a substantially swifter pace now, and Aeton looks briefly at me to show me how relived he is.

My eyes dart from side to side peering through the darkness the best they can in search of a place to hide. The reflection of the moon on the ground catches my eye, and as we draw nearer I am able to see that it is a body of water. The pool catches Aeton's attention just as it does mine, and with a quick glance at one another we set out toward it.

Although the look in his eyes suggests that he has a plan, I am unable to see how Aeton thinks that the water is rally going to help our current situation. We near the edge of the water just as the shouts of several men are heard from nearby.

"Trust me!" Aeton says intensely to us as he waves his free hand over all of us. Then barely giving us time to respond, he leaps into the water.

I follow, doing my best to keep my grip on Clem. Kenina splashes along beside me, her face filled with fear. We reach water that is about waist deep, when Aeton suddenly submerges himself under that water, pulling Clem and I down with him.

Shocked from the suddenness of being yanked downward, my eyes are still open when I hit the water. Expecting darkness beneath the surface, I am surprised when my foggy vision reveals a dim light that seems to be coming from Aeton, who doesn't appear to be holding his breath. He signs to me the best he can to breath normally. I turn to

Clem and Kenina and notice I'm not the only one who is apprehensive about taking the first breath. Aeton mouths the words "Trust me." and I close my eyes and breath in.

The feeling is strange as I fill my lungs with air. It feels cold, fresh and not the least bit like water. I feel as though I'm taking breaths on a cool summer night. Opening my eyes, I find that Clem and Kenina have taken a leap of faith as well and begun to breath normally. We continue this for what seems like hours, and during this time, by the light coming from Aeton, I am able to see the long gash that runs across Clem's back between his shoulders. The water carries away the blood, letting me see just how deep it is.

Aeton looks exhausted, deep, dark circles rest below his eyes. I know that this prolonged use of his power must be what is draining him so quickly. Exhaustion turns into focus as he allows his head drift slowly towards the surface of the water as he appears to be listening for something. Then, his look changes to relief as he motions for us to join him on the surface.

"So you can do that, but you couldn't conjure up just a little bit of water for us to drink before?" Kenina's quiet voice breaks into the night the moment her head emerges from the water.

"Well, this isn't exactly the night of travel I was hoping for, but at least we found water." Aeton jokes lightheartedly, ignoring Kenina's comment. "Just like you wanted, Aella."

We begin to make our way to the shore, when the wind sweeps through and cuts through each of us with its icy knives. Shivering and dripping, we reach the small sandy shore, all simultaneously turning to Aeton for a solution to the cold, but he shakes his head sorrowfully.

"I can't, sorry. I guess we'll have to do this the old fashioned way. Aella?"

I nod and quickly start to gather materials to make a fire out of the surrounding trees. After several tries, I am still unable to get even the slightest spark from rubbing two of the sticks together. I begin to feel the pressure as I look up helplessly at my shivering companions.

"It's hard using just wood, I've only gotten one fire started like this in my life. If only I had a match." I say as I absentmindedly shove my hands into the pockets of my jumpsuit. "Well would you look at that?" I laugh, pulling four little matchsticks out of my pocket. "I totally forgot I even had these."

"Convenient." Kenina laughs.

"Sure is." Aeton winks at me. "We should wait to use them for a little while though. No doubt those officers are still close."

We wait an agonizingly cold and silent hour to start building the fire. When we finally decide it is safe to start, we also build up a sort of tent around the flames with sticks and branches, and decide to try to dry our clothes over it. After it is done, we sit wearing nothing but our undergarments as we wait for our clothes to dry. We put on the jumpsuits first since they are thin and promise to give us at least a little more protection from the cold. Next, we put Aeton and Clem's clothes out next since they each lack a jumpsuit. It takes several hours for all of our clothes are dry enough to wear. When we all finally slip back into our clothes, we each give a sigh of relief. Clem's shirt has a large tear in the back, so I offer him my jumpsuit, but cold as he is, he declines the offer. Kenina does her best to bandage Clem's back with strips of fabric she makes out of the small jumper she had on under her jumpsuit.

My thirst grows stronger with each passing minute and our inability to purify the water that lies tauntingly before us keeps the desire burning. All of our lips are chapped and our throats dry from running and breathing in the freezing air, and being in the water has done little to help the situation.

"If only we had some sort of pot or dish we could put over the fire to boil the water." Kenina says as she helps Clem slip back into his tattered shirt.

"I had one. It was in my pack, but I ditched it while I was running. My back was cut so badly and the constant pounding only made things worse." Clem lets out with a sorrowful shrug of his shoulders.

"Do you think you could find it?" Aeton asks eagerly, straightening up from where he sits against a tree.

"Well, I don't know for sure. Maybe though, I mean, I dropped it not long before I came across the three of you. But if I am going to go look for it, I will need some help getting it back here."

Before I have time to process his words, Kenina has already made it to her feet.

"I'll go with you." She says with a smile.

"Works for me. Are the two of you good to stay here? We won't be gone long." Clem rises to his feet as he speaks, as does Kenina.

Aeton and I both nod in response and watch them until they disappear into the blackness, and the sound of their footsteps on the fallen leaves ceases to be heard.

"You sure they'll be alright? Clem was so disoriented when we were running. I'm not even sure I could find my way back." I ask, very concerned.

"Yes, but you're terrible with directions." Aeton winks at me as he wipes off his glasses on the corner of his shirt.

"Oh you just think you're so funny don't you?" I smile, playfully punching his arm.

"No." Aeton stops a moment and looks at me. "Like I said before; I know I'm funny."

"Well like I said before, you're annoying."

"Oh, good one." Aeton says and we both laugh.

"You know, I know what you did before." I say after a moment, wrapping my fingers around Aeton's. "With the matches."

"I had nothing to do…" Aeton starts.

"Aeton, they were dry, we'd just been in the water. I know that wasn't just a coincidence, so thank you." I cut in quietly. "It made me feel like I could do something to help."

"You're welcome." He returns with a smile, looking into my eyes. "Wow."

"What?"

"You would get absolutely nowhere without me."

"I swear, every moment, you ruin every single one." I laugh, pushing him off of me.

"I do what I can." He shrugs, throwing his arm back around my shoulders.

"So tell me more about your powers. Like why you could create food but not water, yet you gave us the ability to breath under water and then weren't able to dry our clothes, but still were able to produce matches." I say as I cross my legs and turn towards Aeton.

"Well, the king blesses us with a certain amount of power. He gives us enough so that we are able to sustain ourselves and survive during the long, difficult journeys we get sent on. But he doesn't give us enough to go on forever, if he did that we would have no need for him, so he limits our abilities so every so often we have to return to him to get more. That way we never forget where the power comes from. I have only had to return to him once since he made me a Basir, because I have rarely been in need to the point where I had to use my powers."

"What about with the water? I though your power were too low, and then we were able to breath under water by your hand only moments later."

"The king is always watching out for us, and he knew there was water nearby so he told me to conserve my powers and not make any. The when we jumped into the pool, he told me that he would give me the power to keep us all alive while we were down there."

"Then what about our clothes after?"

"We signed up for this Ell. King Fino never promised that the road would be easy, and besides, a little pain makes you stronger."

"And the matches?"

"All you." Aeton winks.

"Ahh, and what about the king, aren't the Enlighteners draining his powers?" I ask.

"Yes, but he has an endless supply of power. They sort of rejuvenate, so no matter how much they take he will always have plenty."

"If he's so powerful then why is he allowing them take it away from him? Why doesn't he destroy them all and restore himself to the throne? I mean those people are going around doing things in the name of the king, and the citizens aren't happy with it. Doesn't he know that they're turning the nation on its head, and making it all look like his fault?"

"Not everything is that simple. The king's power regenerates itself, but it takes time. The Enlighteners never allow his power to get over a certain point. They keep him so ill anyway that even if he did get his powers up his body would be too weak to do anything. He doesn't want this to be happening, and he has done his best, but our nation is lost to evil. Fortunately, from what I've heard the king has something monumental planned that is sure to rid us of that evil and help our nation start a new. I know it's confusing, I still don't understand myself, but I don't think King Fino expects to fully. We only see so much of the big picture and he sees it all. I guess that's why he tells us to simply have faith in him, and trust me that does not come easy for most. Over time though, as you grow closer, his reasoning for things happening becomes less significant, you just trust that whatever situation you are in, he will help you get out of it. He will never put you in a situation he can't get you out of."

Although Aeton has done well to explain, I still can't fully understand the king. The idea of someone so powerful being taken to such a state of helplessness makes my mind hurt. I stare up at the sky as I ponder the information I have been given. Subtle shades of pink in the sky tell me that morning is not too far off, and that is when I begin to wonder where we will go when the light of the day comes. I look to Aeton who seems to have read my mind.

"We are going to have to travel by day." He says quickly. My expression of fear causes him to move closer to me, and wrap his arms tightly around my shoulders. "It'll be fine, I promise! We'll just have to be careful that's all. If Kenina can keep her voice down, and you can keep from falling, we should be fine."

"Funny." I laugh as I shake my head at him.

Just then we hear the sound of footsteps. I tense up at first, half expecting to see an officer or two come into view, but I relax when I hear Kenina's voice followed by Clem's laughter. When they come into view, we are able to see a pack slung over Kenina's right shoulder and upon seeing us Clem hoists a small metal pot triumphantly into the air.

It takes some time to get the water boiling since we are being forced to keep our fire so low, but once it finally does get started I can hardly wait for the water to be ready to drink. By the time it gets cool enough to drink the small pink streaks in the sky have grown, and behind them comes the yellow light of the morning sun. Clem gets some water before taking a seat next to me.

"What do you think of Kenina?" He asks as he sips his water, then passes the small tin cup my way.

"She's great. She's Liridona's sister you know? And speaking of, Liridona was in your regiment wasn't she?"

"Yeah, I ran into her on my way to get my uniform the very first day. The poor kid looked so lost and scared, and her jumpsuit practically swallowed her. Even rolling up the sleeves and legs didn't made a difference. I helped her cut it down a bit so she could at least walk without tripping. She sure is little that girl, and she and Kenina aren't too much alike are they? I mean there are the similarities, but for the most part, they aren't."

"No, you're right. Those two are as different as night and day. Liridona is so soft spoken at first and Kenina sure is…"

"Beautiful." Clem cuts in. I turn to look at him and as soon as I see his face I can tell.

"You fancy her don't you?" I ask, already knowing the answer. "You know you hardly know her, Clem."

"And how long did you know Aeton before you had him over for supper?" Clem asks and answers for himself. "A matter of hours. Boy Aella, I don't think I've ever seen someone more obviously smitten with another person. I don't think you took your eyes off of him that entire meal."

"Alright Clem, laugh all you want. Look at us now though, we're great." I smile, and look over at Aeton who sits in front of the fire watching the flames. When he feels me looking at him, he glances at me with a smile. "So I imagine you enjoyed your little walk with Kenina then?"

A massive smile crawls onto his face, and he nods his head. I find it strange to see Clem this way. His goofy personality isn't exactly suited for love, but I can't help thinking that he and Kenina would get along rather well.

"Enough about that for now though, I think I've already got her." He says as he winks at me, then his expression turns to a more serious one. "Father misses you so much Ell. He tried not to, but he ended up crying his eyes out after you and Aeton left. And Reg, he's still beside himself not being able to protect you. He kept saying that he wouldn't know what to do if something were to happen to you. After what he let happen to Rona and Phoibe…"

"He had nothing to do with what happened to Rona or Phoibe. Oh poor Reg. I wish I could let him know that I'm okay." I say looking down at my hands as I slowly start to twist my ring. "He knows Aeton is with me, and he knows that Aeton would never let anything happen to me."

"You know you have a nice bruise on your face there don't you?" Clem points out, and I instantly cover the bruise with my hand.

"That wasn't Aeton's fault. He wasn't exactly himself. It's a long story." I murmur.

"Short version?" Clem asks.

"Aeton is part of the Basir, a group that works for King Fino, and obviously he can do things that not everyone can, like allowing us to breathe under water." I begin to explain. "Anyway, the day that I got the bruise, Aeton was a little drained from having to conceal his powers, and he always let me sleep when we stopped for a break. He took quite a beating himself that night."

"I've heard of the Basir from a girl in our regiment. She told me all about their group. She was one of them. She showed me a few little tricks, and I suppose that's why I wasn't so surprised when Acton started doing things that really shouldn't have been possible."

"Why'd you run away from your regiment?"

"I couldn't stand being there. They were killing people like it was no big deal, and for such little things. It was just sick. I couldn't stand it, sitting there watching people I knew beaten to death for taking one false step and not being able to do anything about it was driving me crazy, and we hardly got any sleep, every day we would make camp long after dark and wake up long before the first morning light. So one night, we all ditched our uniforms, grabbed our packs, and ran."

"We all? You mean father and Reg? Where are they?" I ask, not sure I want to hear the answer.

"We got separated not long after we started off. They took off to the south, and I made my way northeast, attracting the attention of all our followers somehow, so they're fine. Liridona is with them. I made them promise just before we split that they wouldn't come back looking for me."

"Well that makes me feel a little better I suppose. Did you tell Kenina about Liridona?" I ask Clem when I see her going down to the pool to get more water.

"Yes I did, and she was so pleased she even hugged me. Our relationship is moving right along." He crosses his arms, very pleased with himself then leans back against a tree. "Where's Aeton?"

"I'm not sure, he said earlier that he was going to walk around a bit at some point to make sure that the officers didn't decide to make camp anywhere nearby. I wish we had a little more time to rest." I respond, staring up at the sky.

"We're going to be traveling by day?" Clem asks astonished.

"I guess we have to, we lost a whole night."

"Exactly where are we headed?"

"Scheol, we're going to the king." I say just as Aeton comes into view between the trees. He appears calm, but as he gets closer I am able to see that there is no color in his face, and his eyes say trouble.

"Aeton, what's wrong?" I ask, and his answer is short and effective.

"We need to move, now!"

17

Once again we are forced into the forest. We move quickly, not quite running, but by no means walking; as I would much prefer. The morning breeze sends my hair into my face, obstructing my view and allowing my feet to come in contact with several obstacles. We left in such a hurry, my mind is still far behind, and the fact that I don't even know what we are running from clouds up my mind. I begin to think that our habit of running through the woods like this is getting old. At least this time it's light out, allowing better visibility, but with the sun comes heat. Although the heat is a refreshing change from the chilly night, it sends beads of sweat down my back and face. The sun has only just begun to pull itself over the trees, and there is already such a drastic increase in temperature I can only hope we don't run for long.

I am able to tell we are heading north, but my mind is still stuck on the reason for our running. Fortunately for us, Kenina was able to focus during the panic and grabbed the pack, something that hadn't even remotely crossed my mind as I shuffled to my feet and took off after Aeton.

Suddenly, Aeton stops dead in his tracks and immediately holds up his hands for us to do the same. He turns his head sharply around and puts his finger to his lips, then points to our left. We all turn in unison, and the mere sight of it strikes fear into our hearts.

Its head is turned towards us, lying over its body, which is coiled up tightly next to a large pile of bones. It appears to be asleep, but we stand like statues as we wait to make sure. I peer at the stack of skulls and other assorted, dreadfully human looking bones. A small skull, most likely belonging to a child catches my attention, and I have to put my hand over my mouth to suppress the small, horrified noise that comes out. The air reeks of blood, making holding our breath almost the only option to escape the smell. A small number of bones still have flesh on them, and the sun has already begun to amplify the stench.

The body of the beast twitches as a breeze sweeps through the trees, but it doesn't wake. It looks just I imagined one to be by Aeton's description, and like the one I saw in my dream. Its scale-covered body rises and falls as it breathes slowly. Though it has pulled itself into a tight, coiled position I am able to tell that it is at least one hundred feet long, and about four feet around. Its scales are mainly black, but they also have a noticeably purple tint to them.

"Can we get around it?" Clem asks in a hushed voice, but Aeton's eyes immediately fill with terror letting us know that it wasn't nearly quiet enough.

We all follow Aeton's gaze as he turns his eyes from Clem and back to the snake. The horror spreads to all of us as the beasts eyes snap open in a fraction of a second, and but a moment later has uncoiled itself. There is no way for us to escape. Even the fastest of humans would have no hopes of outrunning something with such speed. Its large, unblinking green eyes are focused on us so intently I feel as though I couldn't move even if I wanted to, as if it's gaze is holding me in place. Tilting its large head to the side it examines us, and it begins to open its jaws slowly, revealing its massive fangs.

A sound coming from behind the snake tears its attention away for a brief moment, but as the source if the noise appears it turns back to us. Two Allure officers step into view, each wielding a large gun. My mind screams that this will be the end for us, and a shiver runs down my spine. The snake begins to slither forward, closing the small distance between us quickly, but as it does it begins to grow smaller, and by the time it reaches us, it has reached its human form. A man of no more than thirty-five now stands before us. The shapes of muscles are visible through the tight sleeves of his suit jacket that is the same majestic purple color that the sun brought out in his scales.

"Well, well, well. What do we have here? Runaways? Deserters of his majesties army? Surely not." His voice is gruff, and his harsh tone is fringed with sick delight. "You know what happens to those who disrespect authority don't you?"

My face hardens as the man steps in front of me and asks his question. He looks over my face, landing on my eyes. He stares at me a moment before placing his hand on my bruised cheek, and then tilting his head slightly he continues.

"Mmmm…They die." His words are short, and the way he says them in a whisper gives them an eerie feel. "And die you shall. Unless or course, you were to come with me. I know you all know what I am, and you could be one too. Imagine the power that you could have." As he says this, the Enlightener turns and holds his hand out towards a tree. It instantly begins to quake, and then in the next moment breaks down the middle and falls away from us, shaking the ground as it does. The Allure officers duck away from it as it comes down rather close to where they stand.

"That is just the start of what you could do, I mean really that's nothing." The Enlightener says, then turns back to me and offers his hand to me. "My name's Dunstin, by the way, love. You look like one who would be well suited for a position of power. Join me?"

"She won't be going anywhere with the likes of you."

I am shocked to hear Aeton's voice, and Dunstin seems to be as well for he turns and moves to face Aeton.

"Oh really?" He says harshly.

"Really." Aeton says back with an equally harsh tone. They stand looking at each other for a moment before Dunstin lets out a sick laugh.

"You think you're brave do you boy? I don't think you understand the extent of my power. I could kill you in an instant, and I wouldn't even break a sweat." Dunstin pauses. "Watch."

He turns then to the Allure officers and holding out his hand, suddenly lifts one of them into the air, and slams him against a nearby tree. The officer's hands fly to his throat as he struggles to breathe. Dunstin opens his mouth, and a black cloud of smoke emerges from his lips. It goes out into the air and begins to take the form of a snake, as it gets closer to the officer. The officer's hands fall to his sides now, and his mouth and eyes are open as wide as they can go. The snake winds around the man's throat before diving into his open mouth. The officer chokes and struggles, convulsing against the tree. A white foam starts to form in the officer's mouth, and in the next moment the black snake come back out of the man through his chest. The back of the snake in coiled around a yellow glowing ball. Dunstin opens his mouth once more to receive the snake. He closes his eyes and his body shakes a moment, and his face changes, becoming younger. The body of the officer falls from the tree into a heap on the ground, and the other

Allure officer moves his back against a tree to be as far away from Dunstin as possible.

"You still feel so brave boy?" Dunstin asks with a sick grin.

"Bravery does not come from sick acts like you just committed, nor can such an act steal the bravery of another man." Aeton says with a hard expression, and it makes my heart leap in fear for him after seeing what Dunstin could do.

"You think yourself a man do you?" Dustin laughs. "You're a boy. Really, how old are you?"

"Eighteen and still more a man than you'll ever be." Aeton snaps. "I know about you. You base manhood off of the number of victims you have, and the terrible ways in which you use your power."

"Oh now you've really gone and hurt my feelings. Really is that any way to treat someone you just met?" Dunstin says, feigning offense. "Oh, trust me, I know about you too boy. It's Aeton, isn't it? Filthy Basir trash, that's what you are. Arrogant fools, you walk around and think we don't know about your secret little band of disgraces. Your powers couldn't take out a fly, while I have the power to kill hundreds of men, yet you challenge me. You think that you're brave?

You think that you're going to make one shred of a difference? No, no, don't answer that, I'll make things easy for you. The answer is no. The only way you would make a difference would be as an Enlightener. His majesty seems to be simply filled to the brim with delusions recently. Old fool mumbles all day long, bunch of nonsense it is. Yet he has trash like you that stay loyal to 'em, and for what, a little power so you can run around and live maybe a little longer than your average fool? Damon gives each of us plenty of powers so that we may do extraordinary things. Take our ability to transform for instance. I'd like to see you do that, turn into a powerful beast and give yourself longer life by feasting on the souls of others." Kenina gasps at Dunstin's words and he turns to her, amused at her reaction.

"You didn't know that's what I was doing to our Allure friend over there, love? It's true though. Each soul I devour simply adds to my years. By now I will at least live one hundred years longer than you." Dustin points to the body of the Allure officer. "Including him, that will actually be one hundred and thirty-five. Oh, and Aeton, you will be glad to know that Maiara didn't die in vain. That is your sweet little sister's name, yeah?" Dunstin pauses briefly to take in Aeton's reaction before going on. "That's what I thought. Well, her years will be put to great use, along with the rest of those little useless brats."

The smile that forms on Dunstin's face makes me feel sick. I take hold on Aeton's hand and look to him to give him whatever comfort I can, but his eyes are glued to the ground. He only raises his eyes when Dunstin forces his face upwards with his hand.

"Aww. Now don't cry, your girl won't like that tuff guy." Dunstin snarls, turning to the officer who has been leaning on a far tree, but he straightens up immediately upon being looked to. "Lucky thing you came along. I don't feel much like wasting my powers on this lot. Pity isn't it? You made it all the way into Aject and in vain. " He takes a long look at us before finishing. "Shoot them."

I close my eyes instantly and secure my hand in Aeton's, squeezing it tightly as I brace myself for the end. I hear the sound of the officer's footstep as he walks over so he can face us, followed by the sound of Dunstin moving out of the way. Then the sound of gunshots fills the air and my heart races as I figure he must be starting on the other end of our short line with Kenina then moving onto Clem, then to Aeton and finally me. The whole world seems to slow down as the resounding of the shots continues. My mind travels to each of my family members. How much they mean to me, and how badly I wish I could be with them all once more. I wish I could make Koen smile one more time and spend one more day working alongside my father. I long for a day with my mother learning to read, and an afternoon with Clem filled with laughter. Lastly I think of Reg, and I want so badly to have one more hunting lesson from him, as bad as Reg could act sometimes, something about him changed when he was sharing something he loved with me. Thoughts of the forest take my mind to Aeton. The short amount of time that I have spent with him has been the best time of my life, and the thought of losing him now rips my heart clean out of my chest.

Tightening my grip on his hand I try to shake the sad thoughts from my mind and focus on all the happy times that I have had in my short life in order to make sure I leave this world with a positive thought as my last. But, to my surprise though the gunshots cease, and I feel the warmth of Aeton's hand, and I know we are both alive. I still open my eyes with extreme caution, and what I see takes my breath away.

18

There, lying in a bloody heap before us is Dunstin, betrayal plastered on his dirty face. Patches of his face and hands are covered in scales as though he was attempting to return to his snake form when the officer shot him. Overcome with relief and joy I drop to my knees and put my head in my hands. I sit there for a moment getting my heart rate to slow down before I look up to find the officer has dropped his gun and now stands wide-eyed, fixated on Dustin's body as though he still can't believe what he has just done.

"You saved us." I mutter quietly.

"Don't mention it." He says sharply, in the northern accent that is becoming slowly more familiar, finally taking his eyes off the body.

"Thank…" I start.

"I said don't mention it! I mean it!" The officer cuts in.

"Someone will have heard the gunshots." Aeton cuts in to try and break up the tension. "I saw a group of other officers earlier this morning, and I stuck around to see if I could catch any word of their plans. They mentioned moving the north, so I came back to our camp and we've spent our time trying to create as much distance between them and us as possible. We've been moving quickly, but with the training those officers go through…"

"I know about the training. We need to get moving. But first, quickly I'd be likin' to know whom I'm travelin' with. I'm Callum, and you?" The officer says pointing at first to Kenina, who is still standing in shock with her eyes fixated on Dunstin.

"Oh, um, sorry. Kenina." As she says her name, Callum examines her then points to Clem.

"Clem." Callum nods in approval before looking to me.

"Aella." I say softly, still intimidated by the fact that Callum has neglected to remove his helmet and mask that covers the majority of his face, leaving only his eyes and mouth visible.

"Aeton." Aeton says before Callum can acknowledge him, causing Callum to pause a moment before nodding and retrieving his gun.

"Well come on then." Callum says as he begins to walk.

"You don't exactly know where we're going." Kenina says defiantly, obviously unsure of him.

"Oh don't I missy? Scheol be where you headed, am I right?"

"Uh…" Kenina is obviously as shocked by his reply, as am I.

"Right. Shall be off then?" He says gesturing forward. "We'll take a round about route. That way we don't have to move as fast." Callum suggests, and Aeton nods his approval.

"Will you be removing that mask?" Kenina says, crossing her arms tightly over her chest.

"Look missy," Callum says stepping towards Kenina and moving his face in close to hers. "I don't know about you, but I would not really be likin' to get shot when that group of officers get here, but if that's what you fancy then by all means. Why don't I take off my mask and all my gear and we can all sit 'round a nice campfire and get to know each other, perhaps share a meal even. That would surly mean us all gettin' killed, but at least then we could all die together as friends, sound good to you?"

I can't help but smile as Callum leaves Kenina speechless, something I had not seen until now. Although she has obviously lost their short argument, Kenina refuses to be beat, so she defiantly starts off, followed by an amused Callum, who rolls his eyes.

We begin to move quickly along. Aeton makes his way up to the front of our small pack to walk alongside Callum, and they begin to talk. Curiosity forces me to pick up my pace and follow close enough behind them so I can listen in on their conversation. I am still a little unsure of our new companion and wish to find out a little more about him if I can.

"You know how to get there undetected?" I hear Aeton say as I come up behind them.

"Yeah it's an old tunnel system for Allure officers, takes you right to the palace wall."

"And you're sure you can get all of us through?"

"Not entirely, still workin' out the details of that one. We've got time before we get there to get everything sorted. What I have so far is to take you in as prisoners, there ain't much security there so I can't see it bein' too much of a problem getting' the lot of ya' in there.

Those girls are goin' to need to get rid of the jumpsuits though. I think they'll take it kinder if you just ran away from home rather than the army."

"Won't they be suspicious, I mean since we are all of age to have been enlisted?" Aeton says, seemingly concerned about how well Callum's plan is going to work.

"I'll say you ran before the army was formed. You'll need to ditch the pack that you've got. We can stop just before dark and take out whatever useful provisions there are. We should hit the closest entrance to the tunnel system not long after nightfall."

"You know a place along the way we can stop safely?"

"It ain't much, but at least it's somethin'." Callum seems slightly distant when he mentions our potential hideout, but he doesn't let his emotions show long before looking over his shoulder at me.

"Would you care to join us, or are you just going to continue walkin' behind us and pretendin' we don't know you're there?"

Callum's words surprise me, and I can't respond. My cheeks grow red and hot as I hang my head in embarrassment. Aeton joins in with Callum as they laugh and continue walking. I decide to drop back to walk with Kenina and share the things I picked up from the conversation with her. Clem has been walking with her, but I send him up to walk with the other boys.

"He's arrogant, that's obviously why I can't stand him. Arrogant people, especially arrogant men and I do not get along." Kenina says to me as Clem reaches Callum and Aeton, and I don't have to give a second thought to whom she is referring.

"Wow." I say looking at her. "You fancy him that much?"

"What? Do I fancy him? You're insane Aella." She says back, but her smile says otherwise.

"You do realize you don't really know him? And on that topic, you haven't really seen him either." I laugh.

"Oh, shut up." Kenina retorts playfully.

"He could be ugly for all you know." I tell her.

"Or not." She smiles back, her voice filled with hopefulness.

"So I heard Callum and Aeton speaking about how we'll we stopping just before dark and then we'll move on to the entrance to some sort of tunnel just after nightfall that is going to take us straight to the palace." I say, now more serious.

"Well, he seems helpful" Kenina smiles.

"He seems a little full of it if you ask me." I smile back.

We spend the next couple of hours running off and on, the heat of the day taking my breath away. Although we were able to get Clem's water jug filled up before we left our makeshift camp earlier, with all of us sharing, the full jug quickly ends up going dry. Only when the sun starts to set does the running begin to seem like less of a chore. While we run I try to figure Callum out. My mind is still leery of his intentions, but my heart if filled with an overwhelming trust that I can't quite explain. My head tells me over and over that he is an Allure and couldn't possibly be trusted as he is part of the same group of hostile men forcing us into battle. But I also think back to the Allure men that saved us from the beasts in the Melaine Forest, and know that there is at least some kindness in them.

As the sun begins to fall in the sky, I keep wondering when we are going to stop, and it feels like forever before Callum points to a hill that lies to the right of us.

"Just up there, and we can stop." His voice sounds exhausted, and I imagine he must be dying under all the many layers of his uniform.

When we reach the top of the hill, the sight that sits before us is unlike anything I had expected. A large city, but all in ruin, just like the building we found refuge under our first night away from camp. My jaw drops and I can't find the words to say.

"Damn, what happened here?" Clem says finally, staring as wide-eyed as the rest of us.

"The Allure came through and forced everyone who lived here to leave their homes, then they burned it to the ground." Callum says his sorrowful eyes locked on the sight before us.

"Recently?" Aeton interjects.

"Month ago." Callum says shortly. "There's one house they left virtually untouched though. This way."

He leads us through the rubble towards a lone standing structure on the far side of what I imagine was once a beautiful city. I look around as we walk, my eyes examining every inch of debris. My heart aches at the sight. I spot pieces of various items that survived the harsh end that came to the poor city. Each piece tells the story of the family that once lived there. Portions of family portraits, metal frames of beds, some small, others large are spread about everywhere. From what I can tell those who lived in this city were exceptionally wealthy, much more so than the richest family in Woden. The pain that these people must have felt to see everything that they knew and worked for go up in flames breaks my heart, and I can't help but wonder where they all are now.

Finally, we reach the house that Callum has been leading us to. It is not a particularly grand house. In fact, it appears as though it would have been substantially smaller than those surrounding it. Three short steps lead to a small porch that is lined with a once-white fence, but now black smudges taint it. A screen door hangs only by its top hinge from a cracked doorframe. The black paint on the house has begun to peel away revealing a once blue coat. When Callum reaches the front of the house he tears the screen door away from the frame and discards it thoughtlessly to the side.

Compared to its outside, the inside of the house is in beautiful condition. Beautiful furniture is placed precisely around the various rooms that all open up to one another, making the home feel bigger than it is. To the left side of the room is a staircase with a banister made of uniquely carved wood. Upon the wooden stairs lies a beautiful blue rug that bends with the stairs as they climb slowly upwards. It is dark in the house, with the only light coming in through the windows and the last rays of sunshine hold onto the horizon. As the sun shines through the windows on the rear side of the house I notice they are each made of beautiful colored glass, and each of them casts a unique shadow along the wall.

"Would you lot mind actually spendin' the night here? I think we may be better off havin' a full nights sleep before we set off in the tunnels. There's not much room to stop down there, and it's too hot to stop for long anyway. Don't worry, we'll be perfectly safe here, this city is deserted, and it's off the beaten path quite a ways, and besides, practically everyone in the nation is at war. I don't mind takin' first watch if it would make you feel safer." Callum offers as he walks slowly around the various rooms, taking in everything as he goes.

"Fine by me. I'll take the second watch. Clem, you up for taking the third?" Aeton answers after looking to each of us for a nod of approval.

"Sure." Clem says as he looks through each of the cabinets in the kitchen.

"Shall we go through the pack now?" Aeton gestures to Clem's pack that he has set down on the small sofa. "Hopefully there's some food, we haven't eaten in a good while."

Callum nods and makes his way to the pack. He begins to remove his mask and helmet, and when he does for the first time we are able to see how truly young he is. Although his body is large and muscular and would suggest that he is at least a man in his late twenties, his face still has a youthful glow, somewhat hardened but youthful. He is handsome, to say the least, with his tan skin, light hair and blue-green eyes that shoot straight though you. Slowly he begins to walk forward to go through the pack, Aeton and Clem join him as Kenina and I still stand speechless, but after a moment we decide to explore the rest of the downstairs.

"Well, he certainly isn't ugly." Kenina whispers to me as we leave the room.

"No kidding." I laugh softly.

Everything in the house seems to tell a story, the walls, the furniture, the windows, all have something to say. While Kenina looks through the small kitchen, I make my way into what appears to have been the office on the opposite side of the house.

There is nothing much in the room, a small wooden desk, a chair, and a few long shelves covered in books. I begin to look over the books, fascinated by the sheer number of them. In my lifetime, I have only seen about four books, all of which had been in a shop window in town, but I had never actually gotten to hold, or look inside one. As I look over their bindings, I try my best to read as many of the titles as I can manage.

Next, I make my way to the desk. The top of it is wiped clean with the exception of a single small blue lamp. There are two drawers in the desk, and I struggle a moment to get the first open, only to find it empty, and the same thing happens with the second. Disappointed, I turn to leave the room, when a metal box decorated with roses catches my eye from where it sits on a small chair in the corner of the room. I make my way over to it and kneel down. As I throw open the small lid, I am overjoyed to find a small stack of photographs, something else I hadn't seen too many of in my short life.

The first picture is that of a man and woman standing in front of the house, which looks much more lively and homey that is does now. The woman in the picture is beautiful, she has bright blue eyes and a sweet, inviting smile. She and the man stand close to one another. He is looking at her with a glimmer of love in his eyes. The house is blue in the picture, and decorative shutters border the windows. They look so happy, I can't help but smile as I wonder what their story is.

I set that photo down and take a look at the next one, which shows the woman from the first picture sitting on the stairs with a baby boy on her lap. She is holding up his small hand to wave at the camera and smiling at his young face.

The next picture shows the boy, now grown up a little, cooking with his father in the kitchen. As I set the photos back in the box, I notice one I missed lying face down in the box. When I pick it up I recognize the boy from the other pictures, now about eight standing with his mother and father in front of the house, but next to him stands a boy of about five or six whose face is turned slightly to the side so it is hard to tell what he truly looks like. There is also a small girl who could be no more than one in the picture who is holding onto the younger boys hand. I start to set the photo down, but take another swift look, and I realize that I recognize the older boy. I snatch the other photos out of the box again, and it becomes clearer. Footsteps coming towards the room make me jump, and instantly I shove the pictures back into the box, get up and return to the books just as Callum comes into the room.

"We sorted all the things in the pack, and we're ready to eat, you comin'?" He says glancing at me, then around the room.

"Yeah. Sorry be right there I was just looking at the books. There are so many of them, I mean I have never seen so many book is my life, much less in one place." I answer, trying to keep my voice from shaking.

"Neat, huh?" Callum says as surveys the small room again. "What happened to your eye?" He adds after a moment, and I reach up and tough the bruise beneath my eye.

"Aeton and I got into a bit of trouble with our regiment leader the other night." I reply. "I have quite an aptitude for getting in trouble so it would seem."

"I may have somethin' that'll help that. Come on."

I nod before following him out of the room, turning back just once as I go out the door. We join the others and divide up all of the food in the pack except for a pack of crackers that we plan on having in the morning.

The sun pulls its last few rays of light out of the sky just as we finish eating. Our stomachs somewhat full, we all begin to feel the weight of the walking we did all day and sleep becomes tempting. Seeing that I am ready to go sleep, Callum pulls a tube of cream out of his own small pack and puts in on my eye, making it start feeling better instantly.

"Try upstairs for bedrooms. There has to be at least one. Take a candle or two with you just don't leave them near the windows."

Callum instructs us as he gestures to the small pile of candles that were in one of the kitchen cabinets, and then makes his way towards the door to take the first watch.

"You couldn't use any company could you?" Kenina asks.

"No, no. You get some rest, I'll be fine." He answers over his shoulder as he pulls the door shut behind him.

The rest of us make our way upstairs, candles in hand, and find two rooms--one with a large bed and the other with two single beds. Kenina and I let the boys take the room with the separate beds and we head for the room with the single one.

It isn't long before Kenina is fast asleep, but as tired as I am, I am unable to make my mind shut off. After about half an hour of tossing and turning, I decide to go downstairs and find Callum.

Carefully, I rise from the bed and make my way down the stairs, feeling my way along the wall, for I left my candle in the room. The house is almost pitch black now, and I have to move at an incredibly slow pace so I don't run into anything. At long last, I find the door and slip outside, where the chill of the night greets me.

"My shift over already?" Callum says without turning.

"Not quite." I answer, causing Callum to spin around.

"What are you doin' up?" He whispers as I take a seat next to him on the top step of the house.

"Couldn't fall asleep for some reason." I respond and Callum responds by raising an eyebrow.

"Well…Actually, I found something earlier, and I can't stop thinking about it." I say back as I begin to twist my ring.

"Are you goin' to tell me what it was?" Callum asks, lightly pushing his elbow into mine.

"Um. You lived here didn't you?" I blurt out after a moment.

Callum looks at me sternly as an unexpected amount of pain begins to fill his eyes. He shakes his head and looks at the ground then back to me. I put my hand on his back, but he shakes it off, and I shrink back sorrowfully. We sit in silence for what seems like a long time, and just as I am getting up to leave he grabs my arm.

"Yes, I lived here. A long time ago, with my family, but then they destroyed the whole city, took most of the kids away and forced them to join the Allure. I've been with them almost seven years now, since I was thirteen." His voice is pained, and I regret bringing it up.

"Once I got inside the house, I just wanted to stay forever. All these memories came back to me. I thought of my ma' and my da' and how badly I wish they were still here." Callum continues to look down as he talks.

"Why did they leave your house alone?" I ask thoughtfully.

"My da' was a man of high standin' in town. He was the one who told the Allure officers about the talk of rebellion. He didn't mean to, but some of those men, he thought they were his friends, people he could trust. They turned on him, and to prove a point the Enlighteners took all the adults from the city except for my parents, and they killed them. Then they came back, burned the city to the ground, and they made my family and me watch it burn from our house. I didn't know how they did it then, but they put up some sort of shield around our house so that everything could burn around it, but we would remain untouched. After the fire stopped burnin' they came, and took us from the house. Not even my ma' and da' weren't spared. I don't know where they took them, but I can't help feelin' like they're alive out there somewhere. As for me, they took me and made me train to be part of the Allure."

"And your siblings? What were their names? You sister is beautiful."

"Well she's dead, so." Callum bites his lip.

"I…I um…Sorry. I didn't mean…"

"She died with honor. Her death will bring life, her story will be one to touch hearts, everyone will know her name and remember what she did, she shall never be forgotten for she saved he who would give one the drive they need in order to save us all." Callum whispers to himself and I can barely make out what he is saying.

"I'm sorry?" I say placing my hand on Callum's.

"Nothin'."

"And what of your brother then?"

"Dead. It's awful you know, since they've been gone I can't get thoughts of revenge out of my head. I want nothing more than to kill every last one of the Allure and Enlightener scum."

"So that's why you saved us in the woods. I'm glad to know you're nothing at all like the rest of them."

"You must be jokin'. Do you think I went around wanting to kill like this before? Bein' around them has hardened me, the things I've seen, heard and been forced into doin'. It's hell. Do you understand that? I can't even say how badly I wish to go back and die that night alongside my siblings."

"That' not what I meant. I meant that they hadn't been able to change what you knew to be right. You still put your life on the line for people you didn't know. Now how many other members of the Allure would you say have the heart to do the same? You killed that monster, and I don't blame you for wanting to kill them all. When I get the chance I am going to make them pay for the death of my younger brother, and the separation of my family to go fight in a battle that is not our own."

"He was there that night, Dunstin. The night they took my parents away, he was one of the men who held me down while the others took them. He deserved to die. Especially after the way he talked to your friend about his sister bein' killed as she was."

"What were you doing in the woods?" I ask after a moment.

"I was on watch for the group of men that Aeton saw, I was one of the ones who chased your brother the other night. Ghastly thing they did to his back, a man with a huge sword done it to him. But lucky for your brother he's mighty quick."

"Thank you, for everything you've done for us today. We would be long dead by now if you hadn't come along." As I say this I can't help but to throw my arms around his neck, and he returns my embrace.

When we break away from one another, and end up looking into each other's eyes. Callum smiles and I do the same, then before I even know what's happened I am leaning in to kiss him. The kiss is long and sweet, and when we pull away from one another I can't help but smile, but then my mind is flooded with regret as Kenina comes to mind, and more than that, Aeton.

"It's a beautiful night." Callum says as he glances at me, taking my thoughts back to him. "I love nights that are clear like this. It seems like every single star is visible."

"I'm truly fascinated by stars, they're beautiful." I smile as I instantly think back to the nights at home when I would go out late at night just to look at the stars a while.

"Really are incredible aren't they, way they have been around long as they have? Since before The Attack happened."

"How do you know that?" I ask excitedly.

"Well my da' used to tell me stories of one time when he met King Fino, and they talked for hours about many different things, one of the topics happened to be the stars, My da' loved them, and he taught me lots about 'em as well."

"He met the king?"

"Yeah, he had business in Scheol."

"What sort of business did he have that required him to travel like that?"

"Um he was sort of a minister for the city. Every so often he would have to go check in an' give a report of what'd been happenin' here."

"But the Enlighteners are holding Fino hostage, how was your father able to speak with him?"

"One day he said he was walkin' about the palace, and he heard this little voice in his head. He said it lead him to this room that was far back in the palace. There, tucked away in a secluded chamber, was where he came across Fino. Course he didn't know it was the king at the time. He found out much later actually from a close friend."

"So what all do you know about the stars?"

"Well, I know about the constellations, that's what my da' said the stars that form pictures are called. Each of them has got it's own name too. Look," He says as he pulls me closer to him, where my head is now resting on his chest, and his strong arm is still wrapped firmly around my shoulders. "Right there, is one called Lyra. Do you see it? It is supposed to look like a lyre." Callum points to a cluster of stars and traces the pattern in the air as he explains which stars make up the constellation.

"How many of these pictures in the sky are there?" I ask as I scan the vast night sky.

"Not sure." Callum replies. "Could be tons more'en I know about. There are also special stars did you know that? That big, bright one right there, that's the North Star. Brightest one I've seen."

"I've always been interested in stars. I never really knew much about them though other than the fact that there are millions of them out there. Sort of makes you wonder where they came from doesn't it? I mean how can you look at them and think that they just happened?"

Callum nods and I can tell he is now thinking hard.

"It also gets me wonderin' about who all has seen these same stars, and that makes me wonder what those people thought of them, especially the people of old. I wonder if they found strength in the stars. In the midst of a great battle, did they look to them for guidance? There is a great deal of things I wish I knew about more'en I do."

"You know people will say that about us someday, they'll wish they knew more about the way we lived, and they'll look up at these very same stars and wonder what we were thinking when we looked at them."

"What are you thinking Aella?" Callum asks softly.

"I'm thinking of all the times when I was younger, and I would sneak out just to look at the stars late at night. I got Clem to go with me sometimes just so I wouldn't be alone, but he normally fell asleep." I laugh, thinking back to the nights when I would be talking only to realize that Clem had fallen fast asleep behind me and hadn't heard a word of it. "I'm also thinking of my home in general and how desperately I wish that I knew my family was alright. I'm thinking of how much I would like to be back on my street, or working in my father's shop. Seems silly, right? Imagining the people of old to have looked on the stars for guidance in battle and me looking up and thinking only about how badly I want to go home."

"We're at battle too, Aella, and I would be willin' to bet that the people of old wished to return home just as much as you do." Callum says comfortingly.

"I suppose you're right. Well, what about you then?"

"I'm thinking about my ma' and da' and how I wish I knew where they were. I'm thinking about how I don't want to start traveling in the morning and also that I am very lucky I am to be getting' to know someone like you."

I turn my head to look up at him. In the light of the moon, his eyes look even more incredible than before. I rest my head back down on his chest. We both sit for a while just looking up at the sky, then Callum moves his hand over and slips his fingers between mine. I let my hand rest in his for a moment, but then pull it away.

"I'm sorry, I…" I say quickly as I begin to get up to leave.

"Sorry?" Callum says, rising and taking hold of my arms so that I face him.

"I…" I start.

"Don't go." Callum tries as he steps in front of me. "Please?"

Torn, I stand looking into his eyes, my heart still beating rapidly. After a short battle between my head and my heart, I nod and decide to stay for a little while longer. We make our way back to the steps and take a seat. My heart and head both hurt as I sit close to Callum, staring out into the darkness. The chill of night seems to be growing stronger as time passes, and I end up shaking.

"You want my jumper?" Callum asks as he begins to remove the warm looking piece of clothing from his back.

"No, I really should just go inside." I say back putting my hand on his shoulder and looking once more into his intriguing eyes.

"Won't you stay just a moment longer?"

I stare into his eyes, and he looks back into mine. Never in my life have I felt for anyone the way I felt about Aeton, that is, until now. My head is clouded with mixed emotions. I can't seem to stop thinking of all the reasons I do fancy him. Still, part of my heart starts listing off all the reasons that allowing myself to fall for Callum isn't an awful idea. I hardly know anything about him, but there is something captivating about him that I can't seem to let go of. Just being near him makes me smile, and my heart rate has yet to slow down.

"I really can't." I say at last.

He nods and I rise slowly and make my way to the door, hesitating a moment before opening it. I turn just before I go in and see that Callum is turned around and smiling at me. I give a mild smile in return before shutting the door and leaning my back against it. I breathe out slowly as I wonder what I have just started.

19

The next morning I wake up to find Kenina still sleeping hard. I make my way out into the hall when the smell of something cooking downstairs fills my nose. As I come into the kitchen, I find Aeton standing over a small pan on the stove. He turns and smiles at me, and I do my best to smile back, but it feels forced, and his sudden change in expression tells me that he noticed. Trying to avoid any talk of last night I quickly start off on some questions.

"How did you get the stove to work?" I ask, tucking my hair behind my ear.

"Wood." Aeton replies as he looks down at the stove. I nod my head awkwardly, folding my arms and leaning against one of the low countertops.

"What's in there?" I say as look into the pot. Aeton gives me a quick glance before looking down.

"Not sure. Some sort of squirrel I think." Turning to the window he adds, "I saw it while I was on watch last night, well this morning rather. It was moving pretty slow, so I was able to get close enough to hit it with my knife."

"You think it'll be good?" I say as I shift my weight, leaning forward to get a look at the meat.

"No idea." He says as he glances in one of the cabinets.

My stomach is in knots and guilt has a firm hold on me. I can't find the right words to say, and every time I try to speak I stop myself for fear of making things worse. Aeton and I continue to stand in silence with our eyes on the ground for the next few minutes before he looks at me and I immediately grow stiff.

"What's wrong, Aella? Did I do something?" My heart aches at the sight of pain in his eyes and the sound of his trembling voice.

"You didn't do anything, Aeton." I say quickly taking a step towards him, but he moves away, not satisfied with my answer. I realize how unconvincing I had been, and instantly deflate as I realize he will not be content until I tell him the full truth.

"I'm sorry, Aeton. I really am. Last night, I didn't mean for it to happen, I just…" I choke a little before blurting out, "I kissed Callum."

Aeton's face turns hard instantly, and he turns his head to the side so he doesn't have to look at me. I stand frozen next to him. After an agonizing minute he turns to me and nods his head slightly, his lips pulled into a deep frown, his eyes glisten, and I can see they are full of tears. My face towards the floor, I try to hold back my own tears as Aeton leaves the room. I hear the sound of Clem's voice as he walks down the stairs, but even though he speaks to Aeton, he gets no response.

"Not you too, what happened?" Clem says as he enters the kitchen and sees the tears running down my cheeks.

"I messed up, Clem." I answer, walking towards him. "I kissed Callum last night, and Aeton is never going to forgive me. Not that I'm expecting him to, I just wish I hadn't been so stupid. I care about him, Clem and now…"

"Well, Ell, you messed up, now you have to give a little time to make things right." Clem responds as he looks into the pot.

"Obviously." I say back in a severely harsh tone.

His face full of frustration, Clem turns to leave, but when he does he ends up face to face with Callum who has just come into the kitchen. Clem looks up at him for a short moment before quickly brushing past him and a moment later I hear the front door slam shut. Callum watches Clem as he leaves, then in confusion, turns to me.

"What's that matter with him?" Callum says, and he leans in to get a look and what is cooking on the stove. "What's this?" He asks.

"Aeton got it while he was on watch, some sort of squirrel he said." I answer, glancing out the window.

"So what's eatin' at your brother?"

"Nothing, he just misses my family that's all. He has always been sensitive like that." I say softly, and Callum nods, accepting my lie as he removes the pot from the stove.

"So where are Aeton and Kenina? I haven't seen either one of them this morning, and its nearly time to move out."

"I'm not sure, I spoke with Aeton earlier, but I don't know where he is now, and Kenina is still asleep. I'll go get her up so we can eat and be on our way." I say quickly and start to leave the kitchen, but I don't make it two steps before Callum grabs hold of my hand and pulls me towards him.

"So, what's your game? You treat me like you got feelings for me one moment, and the next it's like you can't wait to be rid of me."

"Please, Callum, I never should have come outside last night. I'm sorry." I break away from him and make my way out of the kitchen.

"That's it then, huh? You know I thought you were different." I hear Callum call from behind me.

I try to keep away tears as I make my way up the stairs, but I am unable to hold them back. I stop short of the door to the room where Kenina and I slept and lean against the wall. Slowly I let myself slip down to the floor, where I sit with my head in my hands. After a few moments, I lift me head and resting my elbow on my knee I prop my head up and gaze off down the hall.

"You alright?"

The sound of Aeton's voice makes me jump. I start to stand up to leave, but before I can he has taken a seat next to me. The tears are still falling slowly down my cheeks as I face him. His eyes are now filled with sincere compassion, making me cry harder.

"I'm so sorry Aeton, I don't know what came over me last night." I choke out through tears.

"It's alright, Aella. I wish it hadn't happened, but I forgive you." Aeton pauses, then taking my hands and looking into my eyes he says, "I've fought pretty hard to keep you around and I don't want to lose you now. Never before in my life have I felt the way I do about you, and I don't want that to end. I care so deeply for you, and that's why what happened hurts so badly, but I'm not going to give up on you. You've managed to get yourself into trouble yet again, but I don't expect anything else by now." Aeton laughs slightly, but then returns to being serious. "Aella, I mean it though if you want me, I'm yours, solely yours."

I can't speak. All I want is to throw my arms around his neck and thank him for giving me a second chance, but I remain frozen.

"And I'm yours." I finally manage, and Acton kisses my cheek softly and looks into my eyes.

"Right then. Well, we should be going. Wake up Kenina would you? We can eat while we walk since we're already behind time." Aeton says as he helps me up before heading downstairs.

My heavy heart feels much lighter as I make my way to the room to let Kenina know we are leaving. Before I open the door, I pause and wipe away my remaining tears. But my eyes soon widen as I look over the room for Kenina. Horror washes over me as I stumble back out of the room and down the stairs in search of help.

The first person I see is Callum, who is busy going over the items from the pack once more. I grab hold of his arm, and begin to pull him away the pack.

"Callum come quick, it's Kenina!" I yell.

"What are you talking about?" He says shrugging me off.

"Callum, please!" I shriek just as Aeton and Clem run through the door. "Kenina needs help!" I yell to them and without waiting for them to respond take off up the stairs.

As I burst through the door to the bedroom I hear footsteps on the stairs, and a moment later Aeton is at my side. Kenina is suspended in the air with her back against the wall. Her face is a sickly, almost gray color and her eyes are open as wide as they can get. Her mouth is open wide as though to scream, and I instantly think back to the Allure man from the day before. Aeton runs forward and stands before her, an expression of shock on his worried face.

"Help her!" I yell in a panic. "Don't let them take her!"

"Whatever Enlightener has a hold of her is a strong one, stronger than most I've come in contact with." Aeton tries to sound as calm as possible as he examines Kenina, but I can tell that inside he is being attacked by fear.

"Can you help her?" I shriek.

"I think so, but I need you to run Aella. Get Callum and Clem and don't turn back. The Enlightener that has a hold of her will be upon us almost instantly after I free her and I want you to be long gone. I'll catch up. Now go." Aeton's tone is commanding, but I don't budge.

"I'll stay with you. I can help." I say with as much assurance as I can muster.

"Aella, you need to go. Please, do this for me. Go! Now!"

Reluctantly I force myself to leave the room and run down the hall. As I start down the staircase, the sound of Kenina's screams fill the air, but I don't let myself turn around. I rush into the living room where Clem and Callum are standing with confused and worried expressions on their faces.

"We have to run." I yell as I move swiftly past them, and without any other explanation I am out the door.

Fortunately they follow me, and we all take off in a dead sprint away from the house. Although I have no idea which direction to run, not once do I allow myself to slow down or look back for fear of what I would see if I did. We are forced to zigzag as we run to avoid the charred remains of the other various houses. Suddenly there is an ear-splitting sound from behind us, directly following it is a wave of heat and the ground shakes so violently that it sends the three of us sprawling to the ground.

As I roll over in pain, I see the house, now engulfed in flames, and sending an ominous dark cloud of smoke skyward. My mouth falls open, and my eyes are instantly overcome with tears. The initial shock of the impact wears of after a brief moment, at which time I am able to feel the severe pain in my left arm. I turn my head to the side, and I nearly pass out at the sight: blood, and lots of it pouring from my forearm. The cut is so deep I can see straight through to my bone. The bottom half of my arm hangs limp when I try to lift it, and a new wave of pain hits me full force. I roll onto my side and let out a shriek. Never in my life have I ever felt a pain like this as I can feel my head growing lighter as I continue to lose blood.

"Aella come on!!" Callum yells as he runs towards me and leans in to grab my arm, but backs away when he sees it.

I hardly hear him when he calls for Clem as my mind becomes foggy, and the last thing I see before my eyes fall shut is Callum's face hanging over me. Then I faintly hear his distant words before everything fades away.

"It's goin' to be okay."

20

"Aella? Aella, come on wake up." I hear Clem saying quietly, his voice suggesting that he has been crying.

Although I can hear him, I am unable to move or respond. I try to force my eyes open, but I am unable to get them to respond even the slightest bit. My heart sinks as I continue to struggle for any sort of response from my body. After a moment, I realize that I can no longer feel the pain in my arm, and part of me instantly wonders if that is because it is gone. Just remembering the sight of my arm from before makes me feel as though I am going to be sick.

"Aella?" I hear Clem say again, this time I feel a slight pressure on my right shoulder.

I am able to force another small noise from my lips, and I can hear Clem's ecstatic reaction, though his words are somewhat muffled. Putting in every ounce of effort I can muster, I attempt once more to open my eyes, and they flutter open for a brief moment, allowing me to catch a glimpse of Clem's face.

"Callum, come here! She's waking up!" I hear Clem call out. "Aella, can you try and move your right arm?"

I try my best to get my arm to move, but I can't get it to do anything. Clem sighs and I hear him shuffling around a little. Then, I feel pressure on my shoulders again, and I figure he must be trying to get me into a sitting position. I feel the pressure on my left shoulder lessen for a moment, and when it returns I can feel pressure in a wider area. When the same thing happens with my other shoulder, I know that Clem has had Callum take over holding me up. The next thing I feel is Clem squeezing my hand.

"Aella, come on, please. Please, wake up, please." Clem's voice is even more pained that before.

"Come on Aella. Come on!!" I hear Callum say from behind me. "We need you to wake up."

I feel so helpless, and my head is spinning form sitting up. All I want is to move, and tell them that I can hear them. My various emotions crowd my mind and feeling overwhelmed and lost I begin to cry. As the warm tears flow from my eyes, I can just barely feel them rolling down my cheeks.

"Oh Aella! It's goin' to be okay, I promise! You're goin' to be okay!" Callum's voice is shaky, and so is his hand as he wipes my tears gently away. "Does that mean she can hear us then?"

"I'm not sure." Clem responds.

"I hate we've upset her." Callum continues.

"What was that?" I hear Clem say suddenly, his tone switching to fear.

"What?" Callum asks, straightening up.

"That!" Clem whispers back and this time even I hear the distinctive sound of footsteps drawing near.

"What do we do?" Callum says franticly as he stops being a support for me and allows my back to fall gently to the ground.

"Help me move her! Come on, if we can get her behind those bushes she'll at least be out of the way. Then I suppose we try to defend ourselves." Clem says franticly.

If I were able, I would scream for them to run and hide, to save themselves. I can bear the thought of losing anyone else. The boys lift me and set me down just moments later. I hear leaves crunching beneath their feet as they walk away. For the first time since I regained consciousness, I feel the warmth of the sun on my face, and I feel my face twitch as through my closed lids, my eyes try to adjust to the increasing light.

"Kenina!!" I hear Clem shout suddenly.

"Clem!! Callum!!" She calls back, the sound of her footfall filling the air as she moves quickly forward.

They all begin to laugh in relief as they come together. They exchange a few quiet words I am unable to hear before someone begins moving towards me.

"Aella!" Kenina says. "Oh I'm so glad to see you! I hope you can hear me. You're going to be alright!"

At once, I feel a twinge of intense pain in my left arm as pressure is put on it. Desperate to stop the pain I focus all my might on my arm and to my surprise I am able to wiggle it. The pressure ceases instantly following my movement, but the pain hangs on tight.

"I thought you said she couldn't move, Clem?" Kenina says questioningly.

"What? She can't" Clem responds quickly.

"She just moved her arm." Kenina says back.

The sound of shuffling feet grows louder, and I feel the ground next to me moves slightly, and I feel Clem's hands on my shoulder.

"Aella!! Aella, if you can hear me, move your arm again!" His voice is hopeful but slightly apprehensive.

I try, but to no avail. I feel Clem's head on my shoulder as he grips my arm tighter. His breath is warm on my arm as he begins to sob quietly. He shakes his head in sadness and disbelief, his hair brushing my arm as he does so.

"Maybe this will help. Aeton gave it to me back at the house then he made me run. I'm not sure what to do with it, but I remember Aella having a stone similar to this one around her neck back when I first met her. She told me Aeton had given it to her, and then later she gave it back to him, and he absorbed it somehow, and it healed him. It's at least worth a shot. When she gave it to Aeton she sort of forced him to hold it, maybe we can get Aella to do the same." Kenina says softly, and I am instantly filled with hope.

Before I even know what has happened the stone is thrust into my hand, and my eyes fly open. Although my vision is still slightly blurred, I see the faces of Clem and Kenina light up instantly. The next moment their arms are around me, but I draw back as soon as pressure is put on my arm, which I am now able to see has been wrapped in what appears to be a portion of Callum's jumper, and I feel something hard against my skin that must be acting as a splint. I begin to feel the full severity of the pain in my arm, and part of me wishes that I was still unconscious.

"Kenina, where is Aeton? Is he alive?" I ask in desperation as I finally get my bearings straight, and reach out with my good arm to take hold of her hand.

"Aella, I'm sorry. I really can't say. He made me run as soon as he got me down. He hardly had time to explain or say anything. All he told me was to take the ring and run. He said would meet up with us somehow later. I started to run, and I'd only made it a short distance before the explosion. I caught sight of you all and followed you as best I could. You boys sure are good at moving fast, and I wasn't exactly myself there for a little bit so that sure didn't help things."

I lean forward trying to catch my breath. My head starts to spin once more and the tears come even harder now. Clem wraps his arms around me and pulls my head to his chest where I continue to cry. Every portion of my mind is stuck on the last moments I had spent with Aeton. His face is stuck in my mind, and his words also find their way into my head only making the pain worse. The way he told me that he was all mine and that all he wanted was to protect me, and how much he loved me.

I think back to once when Sybilla told me that I should cherish what I have with Aeton because there was no way to tell when it would be gone. I shake my head back and forth, refusing to believe that Aeton could actually be gone. More than anything, I want to be sure that he made it out before the explosion.

"No. No, no, no, no! No! He can't be gone! No…No…No!" I cry as I continue to shake my head violently, and Clem does his best to console me.

"Aella," Callum says as he moves in close to me. "I need you to listen to me. Do you hear me? I need you to listen to me right now."

I nod my head, and Callum gestures to Clem to let me go so I can sit up and look at him.

"You are goin' to go with Clem and Kenina. Make your way to the tunnels. There will be a girl there who will help you through. Her name is Kimzey, she knows you're comin'."

"How will we find the tunnels? How will she know us? Where are you going?" I ask all together as questions flood my mind.

"I'm going back towards the house to find Aeton. If you travel straight north from here you will reach the tunnels within the hour, and we have ways of communication, the king blesses all Basir members with the gift. I was able to get hold of Kimzey while you were out."

"You mean that you're part of it to?" I stutter.

"The Basir? Yes. That's the reason I've got to be the one to go back for Aeton. Alone." Callum responds sternly.

"Callum, you can't go back. Not for someone who we all know might very well be lost. You saw what happened to that house, its gone. I won't let you risk your life like this. Isn't it enough that we already lost one friend today?" I plead.

"I've known Aeton for a while, and I'm not about to leave a friend behind like this. I can't connect with him now, so he is most likely unconscious, but I promise you, I will find him for you Aella. I'll bring him back for you, alive and well. I promise you that. Now, Kimzey is goin' to try and meet you a little before the tunnel entrance so you can figure out the best way to get through. She let me know that there aren't many guards there now, they got called away for some sort of emergency, but you will have to hurry in order to be sure you make it all the way through the tunnels before the guards come back. On the opposite end of the tunnel, Kimzey will pass you off to Rohan, and he will take you on to the palace. Promise me that you will do what I say, and not dare come back to look for me. I can take care of myself; I just need you to get to the king safely. You mean more than ya' think Aella Jadim, more than you may ever know." Callum has now taken hold of my hand, his tone has turned into begging, and tears have begun to build up in his piercing eyes.

"I promise. But you need to promise me that I'll see you again. Tell me that you will be at the palace by tomorrow." I say seriously.

"I'll do my best." Callum says, and then leaves quickly so that I don't have time to change my mind about letting him go.

"We should probably get going." Clem tells me as he bends down to help me to my feet.

I rise slowly and with a fair amount of trouble. Once I am stable enough to stand on my own I give Kenina a quick hug before starting slowly forward. Normally I would be admiring the colors that are spread artistically through the sky, but my mind keeps rotating between thoughts of Aeton and Callum. Their words play over and over in my mind, and I hope that those won't be the last I hear from either of them. One sentence that sticks out in my mind is Callum saying how valuable I was, but he wasn't speaking only about himself. His words suggested that I mean lots to more people than just those who know me.

Although I know we are only an hour from our destination I can't help feeling the walk is taking years. I am unable to tell how long we have been going, but I know it hasn't been long, and my body aches in numerous places. My left arm hangs limp at my side for a time, but after a while I am forced to hold it against my stomach with my right.

The only sound being made is that of leaves crunching beneath our feet. My head spins at times, and I have to stop several times because I am too dizzy to walk.

"How are we supposed to know this girl when we see her?" Clem says after a while.

"I suppose she'll know us." Kenina answers after thinking it over for a moment.

"I wonder how many agents the king has working from within the Allure?" Clem laughs. "I mean you think they'd figure it out."

"The members of the Basir have learned to conceal their powers. When we first got with our regiment, Aeton sensed an Enlightener nearby. He contained the majority of his powers into a stone on a necklace that he gave me. He kept some, but not enough for the Enlightener to pick up on. I suppose that's what they all do. I don't fully understand how it all works, but I know they only have a certain amount of power to begin with, and they have to return to the king in order to replenish it." I chime in softly.

"Pretty accurate actually. I'm impressed."

I wheel around at the sound of the unfamiliar voice, but I find no one. Turning back to Clem and Kenina they shake their heads to acknowledge that neither of them saw the owner of the voice either. We continue to peer into the trees in search of any movement, but there is nothing to be seen. Suddenly I hear a noise from above me, and look up in time to catch a brief glimpse of blue as something jumps skillfully from one tree to another. I turn, still looking up in the direction it went, and that's when I get a full view of her. She is perched on a branch about eight feet from the ground. Her brown hair is braided across the front, with the back pulled into a messy ponytail. Her brown eyes have hints of green in them and watch us intently. She appears to be about twenty-five years old, and as she swings down from the tree and begins advance towards us, the way she moves reminds me much of a cat.

"Aella, right?" She says as she gets closer and sticks out her hand for me to shake.

Having thought for sure she would share the same accent as others I have encountered from the north, I am surprised when she speaks in the same manner in which those from Woden do. On her back rests a gun, the strap of which comes around her chest.

"Yes, you must be Kimzey. You're from Woden?" I ask as I accept her handshake and notice now that she is in the sun the red tint in her curly hair.

"Aject, actually. Aeton and I grew up together in a town where a large number of the people were originally from Woden. Did you ever wonder why he didn't speak like a northerner?" Kimzey answers as she look us over.

"Well for a while I thought he was from Woden. It wasn't until recently until I learned otherwise, but his accent wasn't exactly on the top of my priority list of things to figure out."

"Understandable. You two might want to lose the jumpsuits before we go any farther, they won't take kindly to deserters of the army." Kimzey says, and Kenina and I immediately start to remove our now rather tattered uniforms.

"What happened to you?" Kimzey asks, coming to my aide when she sees me wince as I try to pull the sleeve over my injured arm.

"Her arm is broken, and she's got a good cut there too." Clem answers for me. "She was passed out for a good while."

"Well, we will get her help as soon as we can. Are you ready to go?" Kimzey says as she looks over us, and then turns to lead the way.

"Aren't we going to work out a plan?" Clem asks.

"I don't really think we need to waste time on that." Kimzey says shortly, but Clem crosses his arms and stands still, earning himself an irritated glance from Kimzey. "Well fine then. If you insist on having a plan, how about this; I just make it up as I go along. There now we have a plan, we'll wing it!" Kimzey says as she punches Clem's arm and starts to walk off.

"Oh good. It's not like this is crucial to our survival or anything." Clem gives back with a sarcastic smile then as he follows.

"Glad that works for you." Kimzey laughs. "The entrance is just over that way. When we break free of the tree line, just follow my lead."

We all nod and follow closely behind Kimzey as the trees begin to thin, and large boulders and cliffs appear ahead. Two heavily armed Allure soldiers stand in front of what appears to be a cave.

"I thought Callum said there weren't any guards?" Clem whispers.

"Two is hardly any compared to the normal security detail they would have out here." Kimzey whispers back at him as she slips her Allure jumpsuit that has, until now, been tied around her waist by the sleeves, over her shoulders to cover up her blue tank top.

"Walk in front of me and don't say a word." She commands pulling her gun around to the front, and using it to guide us.

As we make our way into the small field that lies between the tree line and the rocks the Allure officers immediately stand at the ready, their guns pointed towards us. Clem, Kenina and I walk cautiously forward with a determined looking Kimzey behind us. When we reach the now more relaxed looking officers Kimzey makes her way in front of us, playing up her Allure act to its full extent by spitting in Clem's face as she passes us.

"Dunstin delivered them just outside of the Waldenburg remains. He said he found them wandering around the Avedis lake a few days back. The blonde one gave him quite a bit of trouble he said." Kimzey states firmly using a northern accent.

"Why did Dunstin not bring them on himself?" One of the officers says suspiciously, coming closer to us.

"He had business back towards the Woden line, a meeting with Tarek tonight I believe." As Kimzey says the name Tarek, the officers seem slightly taken back.

"And what business do you have bringing this lot through here?" The other officer inquires.

"Dunstin said I was to present them to Damon. He thought they could be effective as Allure, or even Enlighteners. After undergoing the proper transformation of course."

"You know its funny you should say those things about Dunstin." The first officer says with a mild grin.

"Oh, why's that?" Kimzey says giving us a quick worried glance.

"Dunstin is dead." The officer says and quickly begins cocks his gun but not before Kimzey can get off a couple of shots of her own.

Kenina, Clem and I duck for cover, and I end up landing on my injured arm, releasing a cry of agonizing pain. One of the officers goes down with a shot in the neck just as Kimzey goes down clutching her upper thigh. The officer that is still standing aims at Kimzey and pulls the trigger and the bullet flies from the barrel of the gun. Kimzey throws her arms over her head and lets out a horrified yelp, but just as the bullet is within inches of her skin it is almost as though it has hit a metal wall, for it bounces back in the direction of the officer leaving a gash in his arm. Before the officer can even react to the injury caused by the first bullet a second one enters his head and he collapses in a heap on the ground next to a breathless Kimzey. I clutch my arm as I look around for the source of the second bullet, but there is nobody in sight.

"How did you do that?" Clem asks, fascinated.

"Do what?" Kimzey says looking around before she doubles over in pain when she attempts to stand up.

"I didn't do anything." She continues through clenched teeth.

"You sent that bullet back at him!" Clem says as he makes his way to her side, ripping a portion of his shirt off as he goes and begins to tie it around her leg.

"That wasn't me, I don't have my powers right now. There is another Basir nearby." She nods in thanks as Clem finishes tying a knot in the cloth and throws her arm around his shoulder. Just as Clem gets Kimzey to her feet, her eyes widen, and she tears her arm away from him, using the wall of the cave as support begins to hobble forward. At the same time, a figure begins to emerge from deeper within the cave.

"Osiris!" Kimzey smiles as the man comes fully into the light.

"I'm sorry I was too late to stop the one in your leg! I didn't want to give myself away too soon, I thought you almost had them." The man says as he embraces Kimzey.

He is tall and filled out, much like Reg. His black hair is swept to the side, and his intense blue eyes jet back and forth as he looks over our small group. An even greater surprise than Kimzey's accent is his. Unlike anything I've ever heard, it has a much more sophisticated sound than the southern accent, and it is not quite as harsh as the northern. He too has a gun strapped to his back, but he has several additional guns in a holster around his waist. He walks closer to us, and as he does there is enough light to see the various bruises on his face, the worst of which is under his right eye.

"Who are these people?" He asks, gesturing to us with the gun he still holds in his hand.

"The red head is Kenina, the boy is Clem, and that one is his sister Aella." Kimzey answers.

"So this is the Jadim girl I've been hearing so much about recently." Osiris says as he walks towards me. "Not what I expected, but suitable I guess."

"Fino knows what he's doing." Kimzey smiles kindly at me before taking a wobbly step forward, causing a grimace to replace her smile.

"You shouldn't be walking on that." Clem says stepping forward, earning himself a look from Osiris.

"She'll be fine. I can do much more than your piece of cloth." Snorts Osiris moving towards Kimzey, pushes the cloth of Clem's shirt down out of the way and begins waving his hands over her leg. As he does, the cut in her leg begins to diminish slowly until it is gone altogether.

"Lucky it just grazed you. Better?" He says as Kimzey sighs in relief.

"You're right, and much better. Thanks." Kimzey answers in a mildly timid tone as she unties the piece of Clem's shirt from her leg. "I suppose you won't be wanting this back huh?" She laughs.

"No, no. That is all yours." Clem responds, making a face.

"We best be off, the relief unit for these two should be here soon." Osiris commands and sets off into the darkness, and Kimzey nods for us to follow.

"Osiris, do you have a torch?" Kimzey asks, placing her hand on his arm. "Our guests can't see as well as you and I."

"Ravana does, she is waiting about half way through. They will be fine until then." Osiris answers shortly. "And I thought I heard you say you don't currently have your powers, why not?"

"I had them in a stone, but there was an incident with Ruba, and I had to give the vast majority of them to her to restore her fully. I only have enough to do simple things now." Kimzey says with her eyes to the floor as if expecting some sort of condemnation.

"You did the right thing," Osiris whispers approvingly, and Kimzey smiles.

"I wonder why they used their guns..." Clem says as he watches Kimzey, who turns around instantly to respond.

"The Enlighteners are the ones with the real power. The Allure officers are simply pawns. They do have some power, but only a little and they only use it is when they really have to. Guns are sometimes more effective anyhow."

Clem nods, as Kimzey and Osiris head off into the dark. They continue to talk as Clem, Kenina and I struggle along behind them in the dark, running our hands along the stone walls to keep from tripping up one another. As we travel deeper, the air begins to turn cold and damp. After a time, my eyes start to adjust to the dark and walking gets easier.

More questions come to mind now. I wonder if Aeton and Callum are okay, and if I will ever see either of them again. I wonder about Osiris, and why he healed Kimzey, but didn't offer the same for me, and that question leads to another. Why Callum, being a member of the Basir, hadn't healed me before. I also wonder about how Osiris had heard of me, and how many other strangers may know things about me. I do though have the answer now to one of my older questions. I must mean far more to other people than those who know me.

21

Our footsteps resound off the walls as we travel, and for a while that is the only thing we hear. Then comes the sound of running water somewhere up ahead.

"What's that?" Kenina asks, taping Kimzey on the back.

"The River Evelina. It's really quite beautiful; it flows from the northern River Attor. There is a large chamber not far ahead where you can see the spot where the river enters the cave system creating a huge waterfall! You'll love it. Oh, and you can drink it! Best water in Nirvana!" Kimzey glows as she speaks of the sight to come.

"Wait, isn't the Attor poisonous?" Clem questions.

"Oh, incredibly! But back before the Enlighteners went bad, the most powerful among them, Tarek, enchanted the opening where it enters the cave, forever purifying the water that flows though it. Then he named it Evelina after his inamorata."

"His what?" Clem asks, making a face.

"Inamorata, it means female sweetheart." Kimzey answers.

"Right, because that's common knowledge." Clem says rolling his eyes.

"Been reading the dictionary again?" Osiris laughs mildly.

"It's truly fascinating! You should try it, Osiris!" Kimzey's voice brightens, and she takes his arm in her hands. "I used that word pretty well didn't I?"

"Yes you did, but for now, lets try to stick to a vocabulary that everyone can understand." Osiris shakes Kimzey's hands off of his arm kindly, yet firmly.

"Sorry, I just like finding chances to use the new words I learn. Anyway, the name Evelina made sense because Evelina truly was one of the purest women in all of Nirvana. She was kind and had wisdom far beyond her years. Tarek said Evelina was his only reason for living. Unfortunately, she passed not long after Tarek made the waterfall for her due to an unknown illness. She never got to see his work, and it was too much for Tarek to handle. In his rage Tarek tried to revoke the enchantment and once again let poisonous waters of Attor flow through, but he was unable to." Kimzey says enthusiastically.

"She likes to tell this whenever she gets a chance." Orsiris leans over to me and says. "I'm fairly certain she has practiced telling it."

"Osiris, you're distracting Aella from the story." Kimzey says when she hears him talking.

"Sorry, sorry. Go on." He says back with a grin.

"Still overcome with hatred Tarek tried to make the waters deadly in other ways. He used his powers to create huge beasts, which he called drakons, the largest of which he named Dracul. They were fierce and had the ability to breath fire from their mouths, and stood at least one hundred feet tall, but once they drank the water they became gentile. Instead of bringing death to those who entered the chamber they would simply watch them from their nests that lie way up near the top of the cavern. Defeated, Tarek, then cast a spell over his drakons, forever confining them to the chamber and never allowing them to die. He wanted them to suffer by living forever without seeing the light of day. Ghastly thing to do." Kimzey says with pain in her eyes.

"That seems like a bit of a waste, doesn't it?" Clem asks. "I mean really, he couldn't have just modified them or something?"

"Are you telling the story?" Kimzey asks with her hands on her hips.

"No." Clem replies, making a face.

"Then don't criticize. This is how the story goes." Kimzey says in a firm voice. "But yes, Tarek was a might daft if you ask me. Anyway, that very night Tarek went and began to wreak havoc in Scheol. Using what was left of his power, he turned himself into a drakon even larger than the ones he had created in the cave. Everyone was horrified, but one man among them stood his ground, and used his own powers to take down the beast, but not before he received a pretty fair injury from one of Tarek's massive teeth. He was never the same after that, his eyes turned so that they were like those of a snake and he began to transform into one at times. The man told no one about his transformation and continued to receive power from King Fino as an Enlightener. Eventually, he started to think he was more powerful than the king himself, and he even got some of the other Enlighteners to follow him. Of course, Fino wouldn't stand for this. He banished them all, but while in exile, they mastered the use of their powers. During a fight with one of his followers, Tarek discovered that if he bit the others while in his snake form, they would undergo the transformation that his did when Tarek scratched him."

"So that's how the Enlighteners become the way they are? They have to be bitten?" I ask.

"Yes. It has happened to perfectly good people that never intended to join the other side." Kimzey answers with a tear in her voice.

"That's awful. Can you stop the transformation once it's started?" Kenina is the one with the question this time.

"We've never had the chance to find out, unfortunately." Kimzey shakes her head sorrowfully. "On with the story though. Pretty soon those who had been banished devised a plan to invade the castle. They came by cover of nightfall and held King Fino captive. They started to drain his powers after killing his wife, and locking his daughter away. The prince wasn't seen after the initial invasion, and was believed to have been killed in the chaos. They told all the other Enlighteners that were still loyal to King Fino that they had a choice to either join them or die. There were many among them who chose life, many of them honorable people, just frightened, but there were others who stood their ground and chose to die with honor and dignity. Husbands and wives were torn apart as one would choose life, while the other honor and the same was true for friends and brothers and sisters. And that is how the Enlighteners went from being advocates of King Fino, to his adversaries. It was a hard time, my great, great grandparents died that day along side many others. The Basir was formed secretly a while later, and we all bear a mark that was designed to honor all who died that day. We are the avengers of the broken, a light in the dark, and a hope for the lost." Kimzey finishes her story solemnly, with what I imagine to be the Basir motto.

"What mark?" Clem asks.

"Well I don't know if you'll be able to see it." Kimzey replies as she pulls down the back of her uniform, and Clem looks closely at the mark that is identical to Aeton's.

"I've seen that eye before." Clem mutters.

"On your jumpsuit? Yeah, the Enlighteners know about us now. But that won't get us down right?" Kimzey laughs, nudging Osiris, who simply raises an eyebrow.

"Well that's a discussion for another time anyhow." Kimzey says, turning back to us.

"Aeton doesn't have one, does he Ell?" Clem asks thoughtfully.

"Oh he does, but our marks our kind of like our powers; we have the ability to conceal them when we want to." Kimzey explains.

"That explains why I never noticed it before." I think out loud.

"You may have just not been looking for it." Kimzey suggests.

"Probably true." I smile before asking another question. "So does the water have the same effect it had on the drakon on humans?"

"Not a bit. It was just something about the way Tarek crafted the drakons that made such a change possible." Kimzey answers.

"What exactly is a drakon? I don't believe I've ever heard if such a thing." Kenina says with a confused expression.

"Oh they're rather fascinating creatures actually! Sort of like a large lizard I'd say, but with wings! Oh their wings!!! They really are beautiful creatures for having been created to cause destruction. Dracul is the largest among them, and he is also the most beautiful! He's an enchanting blue color, sort of the color of the ocean, don't you think, Osiris?" Kimzey looks to him, but Osiris does not respond.

"That's truly what color he is!" Kimzey continues brightly.

"You've seen them?" Kenina asks in astonishment.

"Of course I have!" Kimzey shines, leaving Kenina with a rather worried look on her face, and I can tell that seeing the drakons is not something she is truly looking forward to.

"Are they really that friendly?" I ask, enthralled by listening to Kimzey's stories. "I mean are you able to touch them? Do they ever come down from their nests?"

"Oh they're the friendliest! Not many people have touched them though; those who come through this way don't generally believe that they're kind. But, I am a right drakon master. They love me! Tarek only chose to give Dracul a name, so I decided to name some of the others. My favorite is Ani, she's yellow, and her brother is also rather intriguing, I call him Ahmes, and he's white as winter snow! They do look rather intimidating at first, after all they were created to be monsters, but their beauty is found in how gentile they are, and they have such grace when they fly! Ahh I can't wait to seem them fly again!

296

Such power and grace, it's a magical sight! You'll love it Aella. You seem as though you would anyway." She smiles.

"Didn't you mention Tarek to the officers who were guarding the entrance to this place? I thought he died the day he attacked the palace?" Clem asks with a confused expression.

"Well, he didn't really die that day, that's what the Enlighteners say at least. They prefer to think that he infected the very being of their leader when he had originally tried to stop Tarek. They think he is growing himself back by feasting on the soul of his host, and that one day he will take over that body and reincarnate himself, but I seriously doubt it will ever really happen. Do you realize how much power and strength is would take to accomplish something like that? Nobody but the king has that sort of power. They also believe that Tarek talks to certain Enlighteners who are high up in the ranking, like Dunstin. Members of the Allure are really enthralled in that sort of rubbish so it's not hard to use it against them."

"The man was Damon right, the one who got transformed and led the rebellion?" Clem asks after a moment.

"Certainly was, I just don't like talking about him. He hardly deserves to be called by name since I hardly consider him human after the way he treats others. The most horrible creature that walks this land that's what he is." Kimzey says disgusted. "An awful disgrace to Fino and the entirety of Nirvana. The most vile being I have ever had the displeasure of laying eyes on. He…"

"That's enough Kimzey." Osiris cuts in suddenly. "We're almost to the chamber."

22

I peer farther into the tunnel and suddenly notice a small amount of light coming from up ahead. As we draw nearer the source of the light, it grows brighter. Slowly I am able to see more and more of the chamber that lies before us and even before steeping into it, it is evident that it is enormous. The sound of the rushing water has also gotten louder, and the air feels damper. My shoes begin to feel wet, and when I look down I see that there is a small stream of water beneath us caused by condensed water dripping off the walls.

When we finally enter the chamber, and my jaw falls open. I knew that it would be large, but it far exceeds my expectations. Along the walls that extend up into the air are large torches that illuminate almost the entire chamber. The only portion of the chamber not visible is the very top where a considerable amount of steam is gathered, leaving me unsure of just how far up the chamber goes. The waterfall is several hundred feet above where it meets the rest of the river. The river glistens in the light of the torches as it flows through the center of the chamber, and then leaving through a dim opening on the opposite end. Across the river, against the wall, sits a dark haired girl who is occupied with her battery-operated torch that she is shining along the wall.

"Took you long enough!" She says as she gets up.

"Who is that?" Clem asks as the girl starts to move towards the river's edge.

"Ravana." Kimzey answers softly. "Osiris' sister."

Upon reaching the edge of the river, the girl begins to wave her hands about the air, and the whole chamber is suddenly filled with a loud rumbling from up above, we all look up instantly. That's when we first get a glimpse of one. Just a shadow at first as it glides just above the steam. The shadow disappears for a moment before suddenly the drakon bursts through the cover of the steam and starts to cut through the air directly towards the girl. Kenina jumps upon seeing it and Clem takes an apprehensive step backwards. Kimzey is overcome with joy and claps her hands, all the while beaming with delight. I stand is awe as the creature glides gently downward and then lands gracefully on the stone bank of the river, shaking its large head and adjusting its massive wings as it does.

"That's Daven, isn't he glorious?" Kimzey says in delight, and I nod in amazement.

He truly is brilliant, black as the night sky, but with green eyes that would make even the beautiful grass in the meadows near Woden look dull. With the exception of his wings, every inch of his gigantic body is entirely covered in scales. Down the center of his back and continuing down his tail sit large spines that appear to be razor sharp, as do the series of horns on his head. He looks rather intimidating until he turns his head to the side and looks at us kindly with his giant, green eyes, and when Kimzey smiles and waves at him, he shakes his head playfully back and forth making him seem much more like a puppy than the huge beast that he is.

"Ravana, be careful." Osiris commands as the girl takes hold of Daven's massive leg, placing her feet on his foot.

Once she is set, Ravana lifts her hand slightly and Daven takes a massive leap forward landing on our side of the river, sending each of us to the ground. Fortunately I am able to catch myself with my right arm. Ravana is also shaken when Daven lands and ends up on the ground with the rest of us. Kimzey is the first one up, taking off towards the drakon and throwing her outstretched arms as far as she can around his snout that he has put down towards her. Clem helps Kenina and me each to our feet as Osiris makes his way over towards Ravana.

"So what's with the entourage?" Ravana says as she moves over to us after a quick word with Osiris.

She is built much like Kimzey, shorter, but just as strong and muscular. She owns the same accent as Osiris and dons the same weaponry as he does. Her skin is dark as well, and her long hair is braided, hanging down to her thin waist. She appears much younger than Osiris, but they look enough alike to be twins.

"This is the, Aella Jadim." Osiris replies as he fiddles with one of his guns at his waist.

"Interesting. And what about you two? What do they call you?" Ravana says, raising one of her dark eyebrows and giving Clem and Kenina a cautious glance.

"Clem." Clem answers with an attempted smile, and then after a moment answers for a rather preoccupied Kenina, who continues to stare wide eyed at Daven. "This is Kenina."

"The hell happened to your arm?" Ravana says taking hold of my wrist and sending a sharp twinge of pain through my body.

"It's broken. There was an incident along the way, and I think there was a piece of wood stuck in it when I blacked out." I answer through clenched teeth as Ravana is continuing to turn my arm back and forth in her hands.

"What, you can't take a little blood?" She asks with a frown.

"I can stand plenty of blood, it was a little more about the pain I think." I answer while wearing a frown of my own.

"You do realize a piece of a jumper and stick isn't going to help much, right? How long ago did this happen?" She grimaces as she twists my arm again and it pops. "Sorry."

"We were in a rush and had to make due, and it happened early this morning." I hold back a yelp as I speak.

"So you were with Callum then, when it happened?" Ravana looks at me with harsh eyes.

"Yes." I answer, but I am unsure of her point.

"Interesting that he didn't heal you." Ravana says softly as she begins to unwrap the portion of Callum's jumper from my arm so that she can get a better look at my wound.

"Interesting Osiris chose not to as well." I say offended.

"How long have you known Callum?" Ravana snaps as she yanks my arm forward, causing me to squeal as my head swims in pain, catching the attention of Clem and the others.

"She's fine." Ravana tells them shortly. "How long have you know him?"

"Only a day." I answer with my eyes to the ground.

"Then why defend him? You don't know what he's really like. You know nothing of his past, and when exactly did you find out he was one of us?" She looks at me harshly with her dark blue eyes.

"He saved our lives. He risked his own life for us, and he knew nothing of us. That's enough for me." I snarl back.

"Those who trust so easily are normally the ones who end up dead. They're the ones who get betrayed. Do you realize that?

Regardless of what he may have done to save you, you still know nothing." Ravana scowls.

"I know enough. Callum is kind and brave, and the reason why he didn't heal me is irrelevant. He saved my life without so much as a name to go on." I answer in tone to match hers.

"You're a fool Aella. To think Fino chose you makes me ill." Ravana says as her face contorts in disgust and she grips my arm tighter, causing me to let out a full scream.

"Hey, you're hurting her!" Clem yells as he rushes towards me and shoves Ravana away from me, not realizing she has such a firm grip on my wrist, so I am sent into another fit of screaming as I am yanked violently to the side.

"Way to go!" Ravana screams as she releases me and shoves Clem backwards. "I had it under control and now look what you have done!! You're only making things worse for her!!"

"Are you alright?" Kimzey says, hitting her knees next to me.

I can't answer. My head is spinning, and my vision is becoming blurred as I rock back and forth as pain courses through each and every one of my veins. Tears well up in my eyes as Kimzey does her best to comfort me.

"Help her!" She yells at last. "She's going to pass out, and that's the last thing we need!"

"This is going to hurt a little." Osiris tells me as he bends down next to me and takes firm hold on my injured arm.

The first feeling I get is one like the intense heat of fire, but the second is more like ice, and at last the pain stops. A few final tears fall from my eyes as I sit up and look at my now totally healed arm. Kimzey hugs me as I look to Osiris who looks drained and even older than before. My arm is not the only thing that feels better, for when I reach up, the swelling under my eye has disappeared too.

"Thank you." I say softly, but Osiris won't meet my gaze, he simply nods, rises and goes to calm Ravana.

"I should have warned you, she's kind of a hot head. She and Callum don't get along well either. They had a bit of a falling out, and even though it was years ago she still hates him, and most anyone who is associated with him for that matter. And in case you were wondering, Callum didn't heal you because it takes lots of power to do something like that, and the same goes for Osiris. When Osiris healed me, he needed some time to catch his breath before attempting to heal another. Besides, your wound was a little more serious." Kimzey smiles lightly at me. "He really is a good man. He's been almost like a father to me since mine passed, and I trust him with my life. Ravana has been good to me as well, after you get to know her, she really isn't as bad as she lets on."

I nod just as we begin to hear the sound of shouts resounding off the walls of the tunnels leading into the chamber. We all fall dead silent and exchange worried glances as we realize what's happening. The sound of the running water muffles the voices some but we are able to determine by their accents that they are most assuredly Allure officers.

"Why are they in such a rush?" Ravana asks franticly.

"They must have found the bodies at the entrance. Come on, get on the drakon and make sure you have a firm hold on the thing." Osiris tells us as we all being to scramble towards Daven, all of us except Kenina.

"Kenina come on!" I yell back at her as I take hold of one of Daven's huge front legs.

"I can't! I can't!" Kenina screams back as she shakes her head franticly.

"What is the matter with you?" Ravana yells viciously. "Do you have a death wish or something? Get on the blasted drakon!!"

"I can't!" Kenina continues to scream.

"Go! I'll take care of her! Ravana your gun, give it to me!" Osiris yells as he sprints towards his worried looking sister. "It'll be good for someone to stay down here and listen to what they have to say, and if I'm lucky I'll kill a couple."

Ravana is unsure, but as the shouts get even louder she slips the strap of her gun skillfully off of her shoulder and hands it to her brother. Osiris then runs to Kenina and thrusts the gun into her trembling hands.

"Do you know how to use one of these?" He asks quickly.

"No!" Kenina answers terrified.

"Perfect! Come on!" He grabs hold of her shaking hand, and they take off in the direction of the waterfall.

"Where are we going?" Clem yells.

"Up." Ravana says, and then without even checking to make sure we are ready, begins to wave her hands, and immediately Daven begins flapping his enormous wings and takes off towards the top of the chamber.

I close my eyes and hold on so tight that my knuckles begin to turn white. We are moving quickly, and my loose hair blows around my face. Before long we are so far up in the air that when I finally open my eyes and look down, I can barely make out Osiris and Kenina as they duck behind the waterfall, and just before we make it through to the cover of the steam I see the first officer run into the chamber. I let out a sigh of relief only to suck it back in when we get above the layer of steam, and I am able to see what lies beyond it.

Soaring around in all different directions are at least a hundred drakons. They are all unique and covered in scales that are the most exquisite colors I have ever seen. Some of them are asleep in the various monumental caves that are scattered about the walls. Kimzey was exactly right about them being beautiful creatures, and seeing so many of them is beyond anything I could have imagined. It is easily the most breathtaking sight I have ever had the pleasure of witnessing.

"Told you that it was beautiful!!" Kimzey yells as she sees my awed expression, but I can still hardly hear her over the sound of the rushing wind in my ears.

I can't help but smile as we climb higher and higher. Suddenly Daven lets out a shrill call that echoes around through the many caves, waking all the sleeping drakons, who raise their massive heads towards us and watch us intently as we move even higher. I can see where the waterfall enters the cave now. A massive black cavern that is almost even with the top of the cave. Water pours out of it at a rapid pace, before it falls down to the floor so far below.

Several, much smaller, drakons suddenly zoom past us, returning Daven's call. As I follow the smaller drakons with my eyes I catch sight of the biggest cave I have seen so far, and just as I take notice of it Daven turns and heads straight for it. We get closer, and I get my first look at Dracul. His massive blue body is curled up, and his head is facing us. His is a majestic creature, and nothing short of what Kimzey described.

"Get ready!" Kimzey calls out as we begin to get close to the floor of the cave.

We all tense up and tighten our grips on Daven's legs to brace ourselves for a landing. Even though we are all holding on as tight as we possibly can we are rocked violently when Daven's feet touch down, and Kimzey, Ravana and I all end up on the ground. I rise to find a trembling Clem still holding on for dear life.

"It's okay Clem, we're on the ground now." I laugh as I place my hands on his arm and watch as he timidly opens his eyes before releasing his grip and slipping down to the ground.

"Is Osiris okay?" Kimzey asks Ravana just as Clem and I make our way back around to the front of the drakon.

"He isn't answering." Ravana replies as she closes her eyes tightly and shakes her head.

"I'm sure he will soon enough, I mean we would have heard if there were any gunshots right?" Kimzey tries, but Ravana shoots her a look that could kill.

"Come meet Dracul!" Kimzey says, looking for an out, as she takes hold of my wrist.

We move quietly over to where Dracul is sleeping, and I can't help but jump as Kimzey sticks her thumb and pointer finger into her mouth and whistles, causing Dracul to stir and then slowly open his magnificently large, grey eyes. He turns his long, thin snout towards her and she squeals, a satisfied smile appearing on her face. She lifts both her hands and waves at him before pointing to me. I am slightly taken back as Dracul moves his massive head to face me.

"Wave at him! He likes that." Kimzey tells me.

I timidly raise my hands up, and wave at him, and instantly his eyes light up, and he nods his head up and down, creating a slight gust of wind that blows my hair back out of my face. A smile finds its way onto my shining face as my body is filled to the brim with delight.

"He likes you!!" Kimzey says running over and taking hold of my arm, and then she looks over her shoulder. "Clem come say hi."

She says, and we both turn just in time to catch sight of Clem's horrified reaction, and we both end up laughing.

"Don't be a baby Clem." I joke with a smile, and he returns with a sarcastic smile as he shrugs his shoulders and tilts his head to the side.

"Very funny." He says, making a resolve and strutting forward to join us. "So bloody scary…" He adds with another sarcastic look, but I can tell he is trying to suppress his trembling.

"You can touch him if you'd like." Kimzey offers and I eagerly accept, and to prove a point Clem follows closely behind me.

The armor of a drakon is unlike anything I have encountered before. The individual scales, are roughly the size of my hand, and feel smooth like a polished piece of glass, but as I run my hand over a larger area it feels like pebbles in a stream.

"I just spoke with Osiris." Ravana says as she comes over closer to us. "They're fine, that girl is still a bit shaken up though."

"That girl's name, is Kenina." Clem says, shooting Ravana a look.

"That is beside the point. Thank you though, I really care." Ravana shuts Clem down with her sarcasm. "Osiris and that girl are going to be forced to stay behind the waterfall, they heard some of the officers saying that they are going to stay for the night. All our packs are down there, and we are stuck in this hellhole so looks like we won't be eating tonight. There is no way we can manage to get down there, Osiris said there was at least twenty of them about."

Upon the mention of food, I realize we have gone the whole day without food after having left the house before having a chance to eat any of the breakfast Aeton had prepared.

"Oh don't be so dramatic Ravana. Can't you manage a small something?" Kimzey asks an annoyed looking Ravana.

"Can't you manage a small something?" Ravana mocks Kimzey before rolling her eyes and after a few movements of her hands creates a small variety of food, much like what Aeton had made when we were in the underground room.

"Thank you!" Kimzey says brightly, only irritating Ravana more before pouncing at the food.

"What, you're not going to eat? That's surely is nice and ungrateful of you." Ravana snaps when Clem and I hesitate, but, upon her words, we more quickly forward.

We all eat our fill without a word. I feel so much better after I begin to eat that I continue to eat until I get a slight stomach ache since I am not sure when my next meal will be. After we are finished, Kimzey and I walk towards the edge of the cave while Clem settles down to get some rest, and Ravana does the same further within the cave. I walk about ten feet from the true edge of the cave before I stop and stay glued to the ground even when Kimzey begs me to join her as she dangles her feet over the edge. I continue to deny her until she comes to sit further back with me. We watch the drakons in silence for a while before Kimzey starts to speak.

"They fascinate you don't they?" She asks lightly.

"They're incredible!" I say back, my eyes shining.

"Every time I see them, it's harder for me to believe they were truly created for destruction."

"I can see what you mean."

"So how old are you exactly?" Kimzey asks as she crosses her legs and turns towards me.

"Seventeen." I answer, still watching the drakons.

"Only seventeen! You act much older I think."

"Really? Thank you. How old are you?" I smile.

"Twenty-seven last month."

"Wow. Have you spent your whole life as one of them? The Basir I mean."

"Since I was twelve. My parents were part of it as well, and we did it together, but then my father passed when I was fifteen, and that's when I met Osiris and Ravana. He was thirty-one then and much less irritable as I remember. Ravana has always been a little dramatic though." Kimzey's face looks somewhat hardened for the first time since I met her as she talks about the past.

"How did you come to know Callum?"

"We actually grew up next door to one another in Waldenburg. I moved away when I became part of the Basir. My parents and I were more like nomads then. He was always such a sweet kid, hard thing loosing ones parents the way he had to, never truly

knowing what became of them. My parents and I were on a mission,

and we happened to be headed back towards Waldenburg. We saw the

smoke from miles out, and by the time we got there nothing was

salvageable. I watched them take poor Callum that night. Oh he was

screaming and crying his poor innocent head off. My parents and I

kept tabs on him the best we could for the next year, and we finally got

a chance to speak with him one night when they had him on nighttime

watch rout for the Allure. King Fino had blessed my father with

enough powers to make Callum into one of us that night if he chose to

and fortunately he did."

Hearing Kimzey speak so fondly of Callum only makes getting

him off my mind much harder. The thought of him being torn from

everything that he knew reminds me of Koen.

"That was the first time we were able to successfully get one of

our own behind enemy lines. It was his idea to contain the power in

the stones so he could go undetected, he's always been sharp as

anything, despite his limited education. Not long after that my parents

and I got into the Allure as well and after that the number of Basir spies grew and grew. It is hard at times though, orders are given to Allure officers with the intention of being followed. My father was ordered to capture a group of children for the Enlighteners to feast upon. He couldn't do it, and he lost his life because of it, and all those kids still had to die. Sometimes I wish he had just done it so that he would still be here, but the king knew what he was doing when he told him to disobey his commands, and I trust the king regardless of what may happen."

"Aeton told me the same thing, about trusting the king, and he told me to do the same, but how is one to trust in someone they have never seen?" I ask, truly puzzled.

"It is hard at times I must admit, before I first saw the king my parents told me about him. They said that I had to choose to be one of his people. It took me a while to decide, but finally I just decided to let go of my apprehension and take a leap of faith, and you know what? He caught me. The king has been there for me from day one, and he has never once let me face trials alone."

"What exactly did Ravana mean earlier, when she said that Fino had chosen me, and when Osiris said that he'd heard of me? I've never been outside of Woden. How could Osiris or Ravana have heard of me, much less the king?"

"The king knows everyone in Nirvana. He used to travel all around back before the Enlighteners took over, but now he has the Basir. We are his eyes and his ears out here and help keep the peace the best we can. He knows you especially because you have strong protectors like Aeton and Phoibe as."

"Phoibe!?" I cut in. "You mean she's really..."

"Well of course she is!" Kimzey says with a laugh.

"I knew that I guess. I suppose I just never really believed it. Aeton told me that she was one of you, but there was so much that he told me that wasn't true. I mean she lived with us for a long time, and she always seemed so, well, helpless." I explain more to myself than to Kimzey, and as I do things start to fall into place. Suddenly I realize that Phoibe dropping her ring in the forest the day Aeton and I found it so that I would have it in order to save me today must have been all part of the plan. Then I come to another realization; Phoibe killed the beast in the forest. "She's alive..." I say to myself.

"Well of course she's alive!"

"Kimzey, where is she?" I say, with a slightly pleading tone to my voice.

"You will see her soon enough Aella, I promise you that."

I smile at the thought of being reunited with Phoibe and how happy Reg would be to know she's all right. I now cannot wait for the night to be over so that we can make it to the palace. I rise to find Clem and tell him to tell him the news when I come to yet another realization; if all went as planned, Callum and Aeton will be headed through the tunnel system sometime soon, landing themselves in the hands of at least twenty, heavily armed Allure officers.

23

"Kimzey we have to get those officers out of here somehow!!" I say in a panic as I run back towards her and yank her violently to her feet.

"What are you talking about?" Kimzey asks as she brushes herself off and begins to follow me back into the cave.

"I'm talking about the fact that Callum and Aeton could very well be passing through here sometime soon. If they come through the chamber with all those officers about, they will be dead for sure. Clem, wake up!!" I say forcefully, placing my hand solidly on Clem's shoulder.

"Huh?" He asks as he sits up drearily.

"Callum and Aeton may be in trouble, I need your help!"

"Well let's be reasonable Aella, first we need to think. How exactly do you plan to be rid of twenty or more trained officers?" Kimzey asks as I pull Clem to his feet.

"Do you mind?" Ravana snaps as she emerges from deeper within the cave. "I had just gotten to sleep!"

"Never mind that, Callum and Aeton may be in danger." I growl at her as I begin frantically trying to come up with a plan.

"Why would I care?" Ravana yells back at me, but I am too lost in thought to respond, which makes Ravana even more upset. "You don't know what he did to me do you? You…"

"Ravana, that's more than enough!" Kimzey cuts in. "If you don't want to help then don't! Seriously though, can't put the past aside for one bloody minute and help save two innocent boys? They're part of us Ravana, both of them, and it is our duty to help and protect one another! You took an oath!"

"To hell with the oath! And as for innocent, that boy is no more innocent than Damon or any of the others. I don't plan on risking my neck for someone who is responsible for…"

"Don't you dare speak about him like that, and what about Aeton, huh? He's important, and you bloody well know that! We truly need all the help we can get, and if you won't do it for anyone else do it for him!" Kimzey yells.

All of the shouting has caused Dracul to begin to stir in his sleep and Daven is now fully awake and alert. I stare at them for a moment, looking over their huge bodies and just then Dracul opens his mouth to yawn, revealing several rows of gigantic teeth, then adjusts his massive wings and suddenly I get an idea.

"Kimzey, do you think we could ride on the drakons backs?" I ask as I head towards Daven.

"Well I'm not sure. Like I said, most are too frightened of them to get near enough to try and ride them the way we did before, much less climb on their backs. I suppose its possible though." She answers in a puzzled voice.

"And those officers, you think they would be frightened enough by one of them to leave if I rode it down into the middle of their camp?"

"It's possible. They're heavily armed though, and I'm afraid the possibility of them being able to bring you down in far too great a risk."

"Well what if it wasn't just one, but a hundred? Every last one of them, all at once!!" I say as I pat Dracul's side.

"And just how do you suppose you are going to get one drakon, much less every last one of them to obey you like that?" Ravana says skeptically, and as much as I hate to admit it, she has brought up an excellent point.

"Your powers!" I say suddenly. "Use them to communicate with Dracul and make him signal the others somehow! I know you can do it!! The four of us can each ride one of them, and you have plenty more guns so we could all take one of those just in case!"

"Not very likely!" She snaps, putting her hands protectively on the belt of guns that rests around her waist.

"It'll work, trust me! All we have to do is get them to swarm around a little bit and maybe blow some fire to add to the scare. Those officers won't be able to get out of here fast enough! They'll be gone before we even make it all the way down!"

"Oh and suppose they don't run? Suppose they shoot us down? Or better yet, suppose if they ran, and were to run into your little friends on their way out?" Ravana asks.

I pause for a moment before coming to a conclusion.

"Then we will just have to kill them all." I say plainly.

"You do realize what heavily armed means, right? We have four little guns and who knows what they've got!!" Ravana says, getting in my face.

"We have an army of drakons! I know for a fact they don't have that. Therefore, we have something that will surprise them, catch them off guard! And you do realize what Callum and Aeton are going to die unless we help them means right?" I say harshly, not moving.

"Have fun making this work yourself. I don't give a damn for your little friends, nor you catastrophe of a plan." Ravana smiles sarcastically as she moves away and sits down against the cave wall.

"I don't give a damn for your attitude!" Clem shouts suddenly.

"Oh, that just breaks my heart." Ravana says as she looks down at her nails.

"The hell with her Aella, we can do this ourselves." Clem glares at Ravana.

"You really think this is going to work?" Kimzey whispers to Clem, but neither of them are quiet enough for me not to hear.

"No, but its worth a shot if it means helping Aeton and Callum. We owe them big time, they have both saved our lives before, and I'm not about to sit back and leave their lives to chance. Besides, I know how much Aeton means to Aella." Clem pats me on the back.

"Alright I'm in. What's the plan captain?" Kimzey smiles as she solutes me.

"Help me get up on Dracul's back." I answer quickly and begin to walk towards his tail.

"Whoa, hold on. This isn't something that we need to play as it goes. We need a strategy if this is to work." Kimzey stops me. "Tell me your whole plan."

"Well, well. Look who wants a plan now." Clem says to Kimzey. "Oh how the tables have turned."

"Shut your mouth, this is different." Kimzey snaps at him.

"It may help if it was dark…" I think out loud, not paying any mind to either of them.

"So put the lanterns out. Great, but how?" Kimzey says, taking firm hold of my arm and pulling me towards her.

"Not sure, but it would need to be all at once." We all stand in silence for a moment as we think desperately for a solution.

"Whatever plan you have, it's never going to work." Ravana shouts to us from where she is sitting, drawing in the dirt with her finger. "But by all means, go get yourselves killed."

"I've got it!!" Clem says suddenly in a hushed voice. "She probably has some sort of power in one of those little stones right?" He nods his head towards Ravana, who is no longer paying attention, and Kimzey nods yes in response.

"So what is we could get it from her? We could then give it to you then you could take out the torches." Clem continues quietly.

"Why can't Aella do it?" Kimzey asks softly.

"Me?" I step back in shock.

"Callum told me Aeton sent a ring belonging to Phoibe with Kenina to heal you after you got hurt in Waldenburg. You didn't think it took all that power just to wake you up did you? I was wondering why you kept asking for help from Ravana. I suppose you aren't really familiar with everything that goes along with the powers but still you're pretty smart. Can't you feel it inside you? I know every time I get my powers renewed I feel like a different person. Aella, you have the power yourself." Kimzey explains.

"You could have mentioned that before!" I say as I run over and to begin to climb Dracul's tail.

"I'm sorry okay, but Aella, I just said you had the power, that doesn't necessarily mean you know how to use it to do the things you are hoping to accomplish. Stuff like that takes practice and lots of it!" Kimzey calls after me.

"So what I don't have training! I'll wing it!" I smile as I continue to climb higher, struggling a bit.

"Maybe we should stop taking my advice about winging it, because I'll admit, it really didn't go that well for us earlier. Clem, she's going to get herself killed." Kimzey says as she slaps Clem's arm. "Do something!"

"Okay." Clem smirks and then begins to climb after me. "I'm coming with you Ell."

"Not exactly what I had in mind!" Kimzey says with her hands on her hips. "Clem! You're not helping!"

"You do realize there is like no chance you'll make it back alive? Which personally, I don't care, but just a heads up." Ravana yells to us. "Did you hear me? You are going to die."

"Like I said before, the hell with you!" Clem yells back as he pulls himself up to where I am sitting.

"You sure this is a good idea Ell?" He whispers to me after a moment. "You know I'm behind you all the way, but this is a little crazy. I mean you've had some odd plans in your lifetime, so it nothing new. But really though, do you think we've got any chance?"

"Probably not." I answer honestly.

"Right. Then let's go!"

"Come on Dracul." I say as I shut my eyes and focus hard on what I wish him to do and to my surprise, he does exactly that.

"Well that was easier than I thought it was going to be!" I shout triumphantly. "This might actually work, Clem."

"Good to know." Clem answers as he holds onto me tightly.

"Would you look at that! You're a natural, Aella!! Now go get you some Allure trash taken care of!" Kimzey winks at me. "Ravana would you look at what a natural she is!!" Ravana doesn't so much as raise her eyes and Kimzey laughs.

"You're not coming?" Clem asks.

"Nah, you go on ahead. We've wasted enough time as it is."

"You'll be missing out." I smile before I steady myself and close my eyes once more and imagine Dracul leaving the cave and he instantly begins to more forward before leaping into the air and soaring through the warm air.

Flying on the back of a drakon is an entirely difference experience than clinging on for dear life to their massive legs. Being on their backs makes me feel much more free, and I don't even close my eyes for a second. I begin to focus of trying to get Dracul to signal the others, and the moment the shriek comes out of his mouth drakons begin to pour out of their caves and fall in line behind us.

"You're sure about this?" Clem yells as we begin to descend. "I mean you don't know how much power you have, much less how to use it. We don't even know for sure how many guys are down there waiting to shoot us right out of the sky."

"I've been fine so far." I say as I turn around to see that Clem has his eyes closed tight, then I take a breath as I turn back around and all the negative possibilities cross my mind.

"So you're going to blow out the lights and then what?"

"Have the drakons roast them." I answer, unsure of myself.

"You suppose. Thanks, that's great Ell. Super reassuring."

"Got a better plan?"

"No."

"Okay, then don't criticize mine. Hold on tight, we're almost to the end of the steam cover."

I brace myself as the steam begins to thin and I focus as hard as I can on the lights going out at once. At first nothing happens and I hear Clem let out an anxious whimper behind me. Then suddenly through my closed lids I can tell is has gone dark. I smile, satisfied with myself, then I turn my focus to the drakons.

The sound of the seemingly nervous officers voices grows louder as we get lower. I open my eyes to see if can catch a glimpse of how close we are to our target, and I am shocked to see how much is visible. Although I can't make out too much detail, my vision is defiantly better than it has ever been before.

"How are you going to know when we're close?" Clem says in a panic.

"I can see." I reply as quietly as I can, where Clem can still hear me. "It's like when we first got into the cave and Kimzey mentioned the Basir having better vision in the dark."

"How come you couldn't see better then?"

"I could, I guess. I suppose I just didn't realize it since I didn't know I had the power. Now stop distracting me and hold on tight."

I concentrate as hard as possible as we get closer to the officers little makeshift camp. Just as Dracul opens his mouth to begin breathing fire as I am willing him to, all of the torches along the walls suddenly roar back to life as a strong flame reappears in each of them, once again illuminating the entirety of the chamber. My eyes grow wide as the light reveals all of the officers standing at the ready with their powerful guns pointed upwards as if they had already known that we would be coming from above. Not a single one of them has even the slightest hint of fear in their eyes, and plastered on each of their faces is a wicked grin. Then, they open fire.

All of the drakons are sent into a frenzy, flying around in all directions as I lose focus. Clem and I duck down simultaneously against Dracul's back to avoid the rain of bullets, but Dracul is so frightened that he jerks himself upward before I can regain a solid hold on him. As he climbs skyward, I am sent backwards into and unsuspecting Clem. Fortunately for Clem, he is able to regain his grasp, but he is unable to catch my desperately outstretched hand as I am sent sprawling towards Dracul's tail.

"Aella!!!" Clem yells as I franticly try to find something to take hold of. "Aella! Grab onto something!"

The loud resounding of the gunshots throughout the chamber increases suddenly, and Dracul takes a sharp unexpected turn to the side, and I end up clinging desperately to his right wing. I hold on as tight as I can as Dracul flaps his wings furiously. Try as I might to regain control over him and calm him down, I cant seem to concentrate long enough without being shaken violently. From where I lie I am able to see that Dracul's left wing has been torn in numerous places from the bullets, and we are no longer getting any higher.

"What the hell kind of guns are they using that can get through the armor on these things?" Clem yells in a panic.

I look up to find that most of the other drakons have made it safely back to the top of the chamber, disappearing quickly back to the safety of their nests. But a few of them that appear to be in the same condition as Dracul struggle along, while others cling to the wall of the cave, only to receive more wounds. One injured drakon in particular catches my eyes due to the excessive amount of blue blood that flows over its snow-white scales. It lets out a loud shriek of pain as it is hit once again and it begins to fall back towards the ground. Dracul turns hard left in an attempt to avoid the next round of shots. The increased pressure on his injured wing causes his flying to be even more unsteady and puts us on a direct collision course with the white drakon that has begun to fall.

"That thing is headed straight for us! Ell, you gotta get back up here!!" Clem calls out as he comes to notice what will soon be our fate and reaches out his hand to me once more to try and pull me back up to where he is.

"Don't worry about me! Just hold on!" I yell back, shaking my head firmly.

"If that thing hits us Ell you're a goner!! Grab my hand!" Clem pleads as he turns and begins to crawl towards me, putting him at an even greater risk than me.

"Just hold on!!" I plead as I try to hold myself in place, but my heart pounds faster than it ever has in my life as we get closer to what will certainly be the end of our brief disaster of an attack.

There is no hope that we will miss colliding the falling drakon, for Dracul is too petrified to pay attention to the direction in which he is traveling. As we get closer, Clem's eyes grow wider, and our knuckles turn white as we hold on as tight as we can to brace for impact. The jolt I feel when we collide is much more powerful that I had previously thought it would be, and my head spins wildly as I am tossed through the air and end up headed for the ground. I let out a terrible scream as I get close to the chamber floor and I pull my arms over my face, but I don't hit the ground. One moment I am falling and the next moment I open my eyes to find myself suspended just barely a foot above the cave floor.

"Perfect." I hear above me before I hit the ground.

I roll over in pain, and that's when I see Clem lying several yards away from me. My heart stops for a moment when the worst crosses my mind, but then Clem lets out a small moan of pain and rolls over to where he is facing me.

"Get them up." The same voice as before calls out sternly, but I am unable to see the man to whom it belongs.

I instantly feel the rough hands of one of the officers on my arms and I am pulled forcefully to my feet. Once I am up the officer does not loosen his grip on my arms. I exchange a horrified look with Clem before the officers holding us spin both of us around to face the man who has been giving orders. Upon turning around a chill instantly runs down my spin and my knees grow weak.

"Nice to see you again Miss Jadim. It's been too long." The man says as he walks forward and snatches up a clump of my hair so that I am forced to look into his terrible eyes.

He nods to the officers that are holding Clem. One of them backs up and swings at Clem's face while the other holds him in place. A sickening crack fills the air and Clem lets out a terrible groan of pain. Not a moment later the officer takes the butt of his gun and brings it down forcefully on the back of Clem's neck, causing him to fall limp in the officer's arms. The man in charge then looks to the men restraining me, and before I can let any sort of cry for help my head grows foggy, and my world fades to black.